**The Harvey Girl: Fool's Treasure
(Book 1)
by Ann Kimbrough**

Published by
Everything Journals/Novels/Ann Pashak

ISBN: 979-8-9870530-1-0

CONTENTS

For the Harvey Girl in all of us

ONE

WILLA - 1891. AGE 18
ALTRUISTIC. SOPHISTICATED. HEADSTRONG.

Father disappeared.

I'm ashamed to admit that it took most of the morning to notice something was awry. The air tingled with trouble, but I'd assumed it generated from my head, which needed time to be re-acquainted with my body. Our evening out had been memorable and late.

"Where's Father?" I asked the maid, finding the drawing room free of his smelly pipe. I expected him awake by now, grumbling over a newspaper or languishing in bed, like Mam, after a big event.

The night before had been one of those stunning moments in the city where the world seemed to stand still and take notice of our little plot of earth, this time for the opening night of Carnegie Hall. I most certainly stayed out too late, drank too much, and clapped my hands until they felt a sting. The magic of the evening lingered in my heart, and I needed tea to dissect all the revelries.

Of course, opening night was just the start. A whole week of festivities awaited us. We had to pace ourselves to enjoy each day with the same thrill. I predicted others would falter long before I would. In fact, Father almost boiled over last night, although his good nature rescued the moment.

It was a silly matter, but the horse-drawn carriages lined up a quarter mile long outside Carnegie Hall's entrance. It created a commotion, to be sure, that continued inside the Main Hall, which was a crush. It would have offended many if not for the flowing champagne.

Such things should have been expected. The lack of planning bothered my father, but I assured him that no one could have anticipated the turnout. We agreed to disagree, and his mood improved when he saw a business partner in the crowd. Once they had their heads together, he cared for little else.

I did not mind. The spectacle only added to the fun, and more was to come. The music festival would continue all week, and our family would be in attendance—if I could stir the household. The lallygags must begin their day.

The parlor maid had no news of Father's whereabouts, intent on her duties. I decided finding Father was mine. It was not like him to sleep late, but I expected Jarvis would know, as butlers were the most knowledgeable people in my acquaintance. I considered heading to his province, but that was usually frowned upon.

Not that I cared a nit for etiquette, but the older staff were sticklers, more so now that I was of marrying age. It would not help to admit that I felt more like a girl than a lady living her eighteenth year. Before long, my future would be set, and I'd be duty-bound to start a family. Unless I found the perfect gentleman, which I'd been assured by my great auntie did not exist. For my tastes, an ideal husband would bring adventure to our lives. I did not know what kind of adventure since I had not traveled nor seen much beyond a twenty-block New York City radius. I only knew that I wanted someone, or something, to shake up the norm.

A scream shook the crystal chandelier over my head. It was not the kind of adventure I meant, but it had me running to the back of the brownstone. I slid into the kitchen, unfamiliar with the slick floors, buffed to perfection and free of rugs. Fresh bread greeted me, but the delicious scent was lost to a milieu of confusion. I pushed past Jarvis and our sweet Cook to find the back door busted open and blood on the floor. It pooled around Papa's most beloved Briar pipe with its sterling screw tenon.

"What has happened?" I cried. "Where is my father?"

Only blank stares turned to me, and I knew something desperate must have fallen upon us, for Father had gone missing in the blink of an eye.

"We shall call the Constable," Jarvis said.

As he took over, I learned Father came down that morning, stuffed his pipe for a smoke, greeted Cook, and asked for tea. He even lingered in the kitchen awaiting the fresh bread's oven exit, but he had vanished between that tasty moment and Cook stepping into the pantry for lard.

Mother stumbled into the dreadful scene, and her sobs tore at my heart. "He would not leave us willingly," she moaned, and her eyes locked with mine. "Oh, sweet child, he will ruin us all."

A dread took me. For my mother's sake, I must find Father.

Two

Willa

Being naive might prove fatal.

It only surprised me, but I was ill-prepared to go out in the world on my own. Not that my ignorance would stop me. I had to find Father, if only for my mother's sanity, yet I must admit to a compulsion to know the truth. Bitter though it may turn out to be, I would never believe my father had left us willingly unless he told me so himself.

We'd heard from the police department that Father was seen at Grand Central Depot. A relief for sure, as he appeared well, yet it was so out of his character. He had boarded a train without sending word, and his destination was Missouri. Beyond that astounding fact, his plans were unclear. Such a departure held no worry for the authorities. Men traveled from home unannounced all the time. For the local constabulary, the matter was closed.

For my mother, worry doubled. Her nerves longed for a simple resolution. None came. Sitting with her in our morning room, I had only one course of action—blatantly lying about my plans.

"Our world is shattered," I told her, eyes on the Brownfield tea set. Its pale blue design and spring flowers offered no comfort. The pot begged to be poured yet went untouched. Not even a warm beverage could soothe our hearts. "My mind is made up. I shall visit our friends in Philadelphia," I continued. "The Monroes will welcome both of us, and I entreat you to come with me."

I held my breath, hoping she would decline.

The grandfather clock ticked out the seconds, but time dragged. If I'd misjudged her response, I had no idea how to wiggle out of my subterfuge. I need not have worried.

"Oh, no," Mother wailed, "I must stay strong and wait for word from your father. I know it will come, and I shall be right here, as he would wish." Her cheeks flushed, and I reached for her hand. "You, however, should go to our friends."

I finally took a breath and nodded acceptance. My dear mother would never expect my duplicity. "As you wish,

Mam," I agreed. "I will go to our friends and act as if nothing is wrong. It will stall the gossips."

Mother managed a weak smile. "We will have him back at home; you shall see, and then we will call for you."

I squeezed her hand, relieved at my success. With one lie behind me, the next to spill forth promised to be easier; however, I'd be journeying into territory where I had never staked a flag, yet what could I do? Only one avenue lay open to me if I wished to track my father, and that avenue was one of service. It was a desperate step, for sure, and one I might not have taken, but I found the most damaging clue regarding my father's disappearance.

Since the police had dropped the investigation, and Mother was beside herself, I took the initiative to review Father's recent correspondence. He'd left it in a silver tray on his desk. One could say it was there for the reading, and Father should have taken better care if he did not want me rummaging around in his business. To my chagrin, I found several letters posted at stops along the Atchison, Topeka & Santa Fe railway. They were troubling letters promising a treasure trove of riches if only the right investor would join the search. My mother had been correct; father would ruin us all. To learn he was running after lost treasure, again, hurt my heart.

I knew I had to find him before he was utterly duped, or worse, hence my need for employment. No regular service would do, however. A governess, teacher, or nurse could not cross the distance I foresaw. No, I needed the freedom to travel without attracting attention, something almost impossible for a young lady traveling alone.

More importantly, I had to protect my reputation. While my heart might be free to act on any whim, my mother would admonish me if I ruined any chance of an advantageous marriage. The tight parameters—especially considering the railway connection—left only one option: becoming a Harvey Girl.

Many in my social circle marveled at the recruitment of gentile ladies to head West and work at Harvey Houses along the Atchison, Topeka & Santa Fe railway line. The fine dining establishments offered travelers a delicious meal served by refined ladies. Every account I read marveled at the exquisite elegance and dining, all served within the short period that trains stopped to replenish supplies and water.

The Harvey House waitresses were known as Harvey Girls. They'd taken over the task from waiters, who'd proven untrustworthy and caused disruption. By firing the lot and hiring only waitresses, Fred Harvey instantly improved the perception of his restaurants. In the ten years since the change, the Harvey Girls were praised for helping to settle the Wild West. Whether they did or not, infusing the railway stops with ladies from our East Coast cities certainly helped polite society thrive.

It would be an honor to work with other independent ladies like myself, although my mother would disapprove. Of course, she could not object to something she never learned about, and I would certainly never speak of it.

The Harvey House interview process proved daunting yet easy to arrange. Their standards were high, but so were mine. With a wage of $18.50 per month, along with room and board—and the lure of meeting travelers who might have news of Father—the job filled all my needs. I, apparently, filled theirs as I earned my position as a waitress. They posted me to their flagship, Harvey House, in Kansas City, Kansas.

I had a tiny delay before my work began, having to journey to Kansas City, Missouri by train first! Traveling thrilled me to no end, as it allowed me to see some of the countryside and witness the type of people I'd meet working as a Harvey Girl. I must confess, I had much to learn, meeting several remarkably strange characters. Yet, perhaps I was the odd one. My idea of the citizens who formed our nation expanded, indeed, and I am better for it.

In particular, I met two men who stilled my heart. One was an artist who nearly beguiled me, and the other was a rascal who had me steering clear of his dastardly ways. If they represented the kind of gentlemen I'd be meeting through my work, I feared that I'd not only need to be proficient at serving dinner but also dodging male attention!

The first was a man named Charles Gibson, a graphic artist. He showed me the most astonishing sketches of women. I took him to task about his overly corseted ladies with thin waists and hair piled high on their heads. The hairstyle poofed upward in the most gravity-defying way, and it would need the skills of a very talented maid to create. I certainly did not know one.

Charles was a bold man and laughed off my comments. He wondered if I considered myself a *New Woman*—a term I'd heard bandied about but knew to be too political for my set. He decided I was the epitome of his self-proclaimed *Gibson Girl*, whom he said favored boredom and verbally torturing men.

"I am neither, sir," I assured him, hoping he would drop the subject. While several passengers had settled into the lounge, he had latched onto me.

"Don't you want the vote?" he asked, gawking at my lack of fire and not waiting for an answer. "You must look closer at my sketches; you are a perfect fit for the ladies I draw." He plopped his sketchbook on my lap, showing me a bored woman with a pert nose. Her clothes fit her to perfection, and her hair was swept high in an exaggerated pompadour, with a snobbish smirk on her lips.

I had to admit I'd seen his work before but couldn't recall where. Honestly, his so-called Gibson Girl was not my idea of the perfect woman, and I shuddered to think of the sketch as anything a lady should duplicate in their daily life. The very idea of wearing a dress in such a tight manner made my ribs hurt.

"How does anyone get their hair to stand up like that?" I asked, finding it the least objectionable topic. I did not want to offend the man, as his artistic skills were mighty, but his drawings were surely only for advertisement.

"Rats," he said knowingly.

My surprise doubled. "Rats!" I instantly imagined a small rodent with a twitching nose and whiskers.

He chuckled. "Not the animal, my dear; the rats are made from your hair."

My surprise tripled.

"You save the hair from your brush," he continued, "then rat it all up into a ball hidden within the hairstyle's upsweep. The inner structure holds it all in place quite remarkably."

My nose involuntarily scrunched. It sounded dreadful and would still require the aid of a clever maid. "A bun would certainly suffice," I allowed.

His eyes raked over my face, and he smiled, seeming to like what he had seen. "Your hair curls quite naturally, so I doubt you would need to go to such lengths." He assessed me. "Have you ever considered modeling? You would bring such vitality to my ideal of the perfect woman."

"I already have a job, sir," I told him, "as well as a purpose and modeling is neither." I would have fixed him with my most bored expression to discourage further discussion, but he appeared to like a woman's disdain. Instead, I decided to ask him a very pointed question. "If you will, sir, have you ever encountered fortune hunters when traveling?"

He was taken aback. "In what manner would these fortune hunters take?"

"I believe it starts with a friendly conversation," I said, recalling the first letter to my father. It mentioned how he'd met the scoundrels in passing and then how they re-established the connection. "A card game is sometimes offered, but then an adventure is talked of and how a treasure trove is waiting to be claimed."

Charles considered me, and I could see he knew of the ruse. Yet, he held back as if he needed time to make up his mind. He cleared his throat. "Take care, my dear, for I have witnessed such duplicity. I was able to extricate myself, but not without effort. These men are the worst kind."

"Are they still amongst us?" I asked, feeling a rush of hope that I might find something that would lead to them and thus to Father.

"Indeed, they are," he said.

"How would I know them?"

Charles wagged a finger at me. "You must not. Stay clear, I implore you."

"Oh, for sure I will, sir, but how am I to keep them at bay and protect myself?" I pouted in a way that I'd found useful in the past. "If I come upon these men, they might snare me in their web before I am wise to their evil plot. However, if I knew them on sight, I would avoid them, most definitely."

He considered my plea, softening in the face of my faked distress. "They travel as a duo," he said, squinting in earnest. "One a British gentleman, it would seem, and the other a brute of a man. He could throw a horse over a train."

I wanted to see that feat but kept my expression neutral. "I am indebted to you, sir."

"Perhaps you shall also do me a kindness and at least allow me to sketch your lovely profile?" He winked.

I smiled politely, shaking my head in the negative. If Mam had taught me anything, a sweet disposition could sway the sea while turbulence stirred up only a whirlpool of regret.

He smiled in return and bid me a good day.

In future years, Charles Dana Gibson's art grew to much acclaim. I was always thankful for his assistance that day, but I could never applaud his talented sketches, as I would not aspire to look like a Gibson Girl. As it turned out, being a Harvey Girl was all I could handle.

The second man I met on my journey to Kansas City accosted me when moving between train cars. The swaying along the track threw us together. He caught me by the shoulders and held me a moment too long. I looked up into his stormy eyes in reproach.

"Sir, do you make it a habit to wait between cars in hopes of aiding a lady?" My expression must have flared with disapproval, for he released me.

"Only to save them from a nasty fall," he said, voice deep and sultry.

I was immune to such roguish tricks. I barely even noticed his beefy biceps or the depth of his aqua eyes. I'd seen better. I pulled my skirts away from him, ready to move on without another word, but he had not finished.

"I overheard you asking about treasure hunters," he said.

"Overheard?" I cried, feeling a twinge that I'd missed spotting an eavesdropper.

"Steer clear of those men," he warned, "the British one and his thug."

I angled my head just a touch to the side, raising an eyebrow to look at him. "And who shall I thank for such a helpful suggestion?"

His eyebrow arched in response. "A Pinkerton Man."

My stomach dropped. The last thing I wanted to do was fall foul of the Pinkerton Agency. While their reputation was legendary, their operatives were not the sort of men I could associate with and protect my virtue. Mother would undoubtedly faint if anyone used my name and that of a Pinkerton in the same sentence, and here I was conversing with one.

Oh dear, oh dear, it was the absolute worst turn of events!

THREE

WILLA

The Pinkerton Man scowled.

"Drop your interest in those scoundrels," he repeated with a growl to his deep baritone. It had to be an affectation he'd developed. A skill, if you will, to aid his line of work.

I did not immediately respond to his tactics; instead, I counted the train tracks' clicks as we rolled over them. They beat. Their beat. To the beat. Of my heart. The rhythmic pace soothed frayed nerves.

Stalling my answer, however, only made the infuriating man frown as if I didn't understand his order. His brow wrinkled, and he scratched his chin. Perhaps he had an itch, or his morning shave had left his skin irritated, but I worried it had more to do with me. He seemed to be waiting for a response.

When none readily came, he leaned closer, filling the slight gangway space between us with his large, muscular frame. "Their names are Sullivan and Tuck." He nodded as if the news should mean something to me. "They are the worst sort and will rob you of your coin without a clue. They zero in on the helpless and infirm—the easy targets, if you will—until they pick them clean. They have no morals and will show no pity for a girl. Do you take my meaning? Smile if you understand. Frown, if you're just the senseless, silly sort."

I punched him in the arm. It hurt like heck, and I feared all the knuckles on my right hand would turn into a purple bruise, but I ignored the sensation. He'd never see my pain. I crossed the injured appendage under my other arm as if nothing were amiss but his attitude.

He moved back and chuckled. "Finally, we have a sign of life," he said, with far more humor than a gentleman would normally show in polite company. "I was almost certain I'd scared the ghost out of you."

"I want no trouble with a Pinkerton Man," I told him.

"You have none," he replied evenly, until his left eyebrow arched, "unless you've fallen fowl of one of my brothers."

I recognized teasing and gave him a withering look. He winked.

"I'll have none of that," I practically shouted. I'd have moved on if he wasn't such a big brute, but his bulk blocked the way. I'd never get past him without brushing his legs with my skirts—something a lady would never do unless she wanted to draw a man's attention.

Luckily, he realized we could not linger on the gangway but insisted on ushering me back to my seat. Once settled, I assumed he would leave. I was mistaken. Finn had the nerve to occupy the empty seat across from mine.

"Which Harvey House have you been posted to?" he asked, continuing his unwelcome interrogation.

"Kansas City."

He considered the location, I assumed, grunting a bit, mulling it over. "The first one."

"So they tell me." I looked out the window.

The flat, sun-bleached land rolled by at a calming pace. In the distance, a lush tree line fronted the mountain peaks. I wondered how many had traveled this way and if my father was recently among them. I'd taken a leap—although an educated one—that this had been his path.

Traveling came to Father naturally, though. He often spoke of how grand it felt to see for miles and miles until the ground melted into the horizon. The city blocked such views unless one had the time or inclination to travel to the edge of town. I never took the journey, but he had many times. Father had a strong wanderlust.

"Kansas City is still a rough town," the Pinkerton Man continued, insisting on imparting more useless information.

"What is your name, sir?" I turned to him suddenly, cutting through something about the Hannibal bridge and how its construction created a boom in Kansas City's population.

"Finn Morgan." He smiled, showing some manners.

At least he had all his teeth. That's one good thing about him, although I could not find another.

"Don't let me keep you, Mister Morgan," I over-enunciated his last name. It was a minor annoyance of mine when it was used against me. It always made me feel as if the speaker doubted the quality of my hearing. I hoped it would offend the Pinkerton Man, as well. It did not.

He smiled again, which was quickly becoming my new annoyance. "And whom do I have the honor of meeting?" He paused, waiting for me to supply a name.

"Willa Abbot, but you need not take note of it," I said, catching a flicker of recognition for my surname. We were one of the 400, although only Mrs. Astor knew all the names on her list. For the rest of us, it came down to old money and new money. We were old money; perhaps the Pinkerton Man had spent time working in New York and heard of us. I hardly cared with more pressing matters at hand.

"Names are important."

"I meant you won't have the need to use it, as my time will be taxed," I said with a shy, practiced glance toward him. "I assure you, Kansas City shall see little of me except for what comes through the Harvey House doors."

"Almost everyone visits the Harvey House." He nodded knowingly. "I expect they will come regularly once they get a gander at you."

My eyes opened wide. For the first time, I really looked at Finn. He was either teasing or flirting or some twisted pretzel of the two. Neither was welcome. He took my stare, unflinching.

"Sir," I said with a serious edge, "please refrain from such comments. I have not come West for the likes of you."

He faked a sigh at my revelation. "What have you come for?"

I considered not answering, as the man was infuriating, but his occupation covered a lot of distance. He could prove useful in any search. "My father is missing." I let the stunning information sink in, pleased that he took the news with more care than anything else I'd mentioned. "My thoughts are only of him and word of his whereabouts."

He nodded, clearly running through all the steps I would have already taken to get to this point. To his credit, he did not do the obvious and belittle my concern or my quest. "I see."

Unsure of what he could envision since I'd told him the bare minimum, I turned to look out the window. It was intended to be his cue to leave me. He did not.

"If you believe your father is somehow in the company of Sullivan and Tuck, I assure you that could not be the case." He stroked his chin in thought. "They are more likely to take his money and disappear."

"Thank you, I will take all your counsel to heart and bid you safe travels." It was my turn to smile sweetly.

He frowned. "You are finished with me then? I should move along?"

"I would never say so to your face." My stare froze on a point just to the left of his head.

"I believe you just did." He leaned back in the seat, pleased with himself. "I'd stay longer, Miss Abbot, if you can manage the intrusion."

"I'm sure I don't know what you mean." I also relaxed in my seat, unwilling to give him the upper hand.

Warily, we watched each other. I wondered what he saw. For my part, I couldn't overlook the fullness of his lips. They pouted for a brief moment, but our stare-off was interrupted. A noise behind me made Finn jump to his feet and rush down the aisle. I turned, marveling at his speed and agility. He moved like a lean panther, all power and strength—chasing a man out of the First Class cabin.

Without a second thought, I rushed after Finn.

Heads turned, shouts warned. The pursuit did not stop. We ran through several passenger cars, disrupting all with the commotion. The wild-faced man tipped luggage off overhead racks and threw anything within his grasp—even a woman's apple—to stall us. In those moments, I caught his countenance: all flushed with red splotches, red mustache askew, and fear in his bloodshot eyes.

The desperate man stumbled, causing us to slow down. Finn's glorious muscles went taunt. I could see them tightening through his shirt. Rather extraordinary, I must say.

"Give it up," Finn warned, but the wretch spun to the side and dashed onward.

I worried for the conductor or even the car that held an office for the train staff. Any and all could fall prey to this awful rogue, yet when we reached the baggage car, we found the wild man screeching and tugging at the far door. It had been shut and locked. The conductor must have heard the commotion and rightly locked it.

"You're going no farther!" Finn shouted. "Stand down now, lad."

I stalled at the car's door, confident neither man knew I'd followed behind. If possible, they never would. I had every intention of retreating—but the wild man pulled a knife.

Finn raised his hands, defensive. He'd edge close enough to be in range of the deadly blade.

Without thinking, I grabbed a shoe-sized package stacked on top of a crate and threw it at the knife. To my surprise, it hit the wild man's hand. The knife fell to the ground, and Finn surged forward, taking his assailant down. The impact caused several wallets to fall from the thief's jacket. I could only assume he was a pickpocket.

Finn briefly glared in my direction as I backed out of the baggage car. Train employees rushed by, taking the man into custody. I returned to the First Class lounge, hoping for Charles Gibson's welcoming smile. Unfortunately, he'd found another lady to dazzle with his sketches, and here I thought I was special. He would have made a nice buffer between the Pinkerton Man and me.

Just as I was considering a safe place to hide, a firm finger tapped my shoulder. I cringed, more than surprised that Finn had caught up to me so fast, but I was wrong. A cockney accent accompanied the poking, and the voice sounded older, gruffer.

The male voice whispered, "I can take you to your father."

FOUR

FINN – 1891. AGE 24
WORLDLY. STRAPPING. GALLANT.

The chit saved me!

Not that I've ever had any trouble taking down a man with a knife, but the one I faced in the luggage car was rather slippery. All my years with the Pinkerton Agency, though, and a socialite tilted the odds in my favor. Dang, if I hadn't gotten her all wrong.

Willa Abbot initially struck me as New York elite; in my experience, that lot was too good for common folk. However, she had fire and determination and even kept up with me while chasing down a pickpocket.

The loyalty of that moment filled me with a sense of debt. A foreign feeling that I needed to dispel. The headstrong girl, especially one with good-natured intentions, was one impulse away from disaster. I'd only need to stay close to pay her back. Once I cleared the obligation, I'd move on.

Making my way back through the train cars, I hardly knew what to say to Willa. She wouldn't want my help, nor had she fallen under my charms, which I'd been led to believe were quite powerful. Miss Willa Abbot was unique. I wondered how many other women were like her. Was she one of a new breed or a rare creature? Willa could be the kind of girl that came along once in a lifetime.

Perhaps I'd find out this very hour.

It didn't take long to catch up to her, but she wasn't alone in the First Class coach. I hung back, waiting to enter. I could just see the top of her head. I'd know that tawny color anywhere. A man in a green checkered suit stood in the aisle, looking down at her. It was too large, yet he appeared comfortable, nonchalant, resting a hand against the bank of seats opposite hers. The man made my skin crawl.

Not that I'd made his acquaintance. I knew the type. He was after something, and Willa was his target. Part of me wanted to rush forward and haul him off by the collar. Of course, whatever Willa thought of the man, she'd hate my interference. I'd learned that much about her. Stealth and patience were needed until I gleaned the right moment to approach.

What mattered most, of course, was finding an opportunity to assist Willa. I congratulated myself on the swiftness. Repayment for her assistance was at hand, even if the speed caused a pang near my heart. I would soon have no reason to linger in Kansas City. The Pinkertons would take me elsewhere. Funny that... another strange emotion... regret.

WILLA

"I can take you to your father!"

The man with a cockney accent repeated his incredible statement. I turned to behold the stranger and assess whether he could support his claim.

Standing in the first-class aisle, he fought the train's swaying. Feet shoulder-width apart and both arms out to grasp the adjacent seats, he wore the most repulsive checkered green suit—wool, no less. I quickly determined he was neither of the con men I'd been warned against. The stranger was not tall nor fit enough to be either of the men who bamboozled my father. He looked more like a traveling salesman who never missed a meal.

"I beg your pardon," I said, trying to remember my manners despite a welling hope that the man might actually help.

He tipped his cap. It matched the green checks crafted from the same fabric bolt. "I hope I have not startled you, my dear."

"You most certainly have," I said, "especially if you have news of my dear father."

"Allow me to introduce myself; I am your father's business partner." He bowed his head, yet his voice held no charm. It left me with the impression that he favored Father as much as a mud sandwich sprinkled with worms.

Trying to hold judgment, I waited for the man to offer a name. Perhaps I'd heard it before in my parents' parlor. Father had many dealings in town, as he was keen to find those rare projects that required vision and capital. He'd discovered several opportunities and had added to our family's fortune by investing in the future.

The stranger, however, offered nothing to instill faith. My lips sagged. I could not control it as I settled back into my seat. "Father loves to find the rare investment. What was yours, Mister..." I left the sentence unfinished. Perhaps it was a ploy, but would he step up or avoid it again?

The peculiar barrel-chested man cleared his throat. "Ours was indeed rare." He lowered his voice. "I'm quite worried that it has gone fowl, and your father is compromised. Why else would he leave town without alerting anyone?"

I cared little for the implication. "Why would father contact you? Are you not a man to manage your own affairs?"

He'd remained standing, uneasy. The train rocked him, as a particularly rough section of the track made him clutch for a better handhold. He grunted with the effort.

"Sit down before you fall," I ordered.

"I should not," he countered. "I have upset you."

Watching his discomfort, I wondered if I could double it. "My father's reputation is outstanding, and if you wish to stay in my good graces, you will say no more on the subject. Such slander will be shared with him."

"But you can not share it," he said, "as your father has left you as high and dry as he has me."

"Sir," I snapped, "take care with your accusations. I have no reason to take your word over a most beloved father, also respected by the gentlemen of New York."

Biting his lip, the ungracious man pulled a card from his vest pocket and held it to me. I'd have found it more welcoming if he'd offered me a snake.

The card shook slightly, but he continued to hold it out. "The answers you seek are here," he said, thrusting the card toward me.

"I seriously doubt your card offers anything that would interest me." My chin rose. I'd known that many perils would await me on this journey, but bald-faced lies were not one of them.

He waved the card in the air, making a small figure eight. "My only offense is speaking out of turn. The bad news is not my making, yet I beg your pardon. To believe, you must see for yourself."

"See what?" I couldn't look at him anymore. The devil practically dripped from his mouth.

"You must witness your father's house."

The statement hung between us. Every instinct screamed at me to contradict the man, to make him state the accusation in the clearest of terms, but I understood his full meaning. I could almost read the whole address on the card. It was not our home in New York but an address in Kansas City.

The sound of the train car door sliding open interrupted any response. The strange man dropped the card on the seat next to me. It glanced off onto the floor. He dared not take the time to retrieve it, instead quickly retreating down the car aisle.

The countryside blurred out my window, more from the tears welling in my eyes than the speed. I fought, blinking them away. The last thing I wanted was a tear to roll down my cheek.

"What has happened?" Finn Morgan stormed toward my seat. "Who was that man?"

I could only shake my head.

Finn bent to pick up the card. "Are you harmed?"

I felt his eyes on me but could not put him at ease.

He sat in the seat across from mine, taking my face in his hands. The gentleness of his touch was a surprise. The question in his eyes was full of empathy, much more than any words could conjure.

I met his gaze. "My father, I've been told, maintains a second residence."

The implication caused him to lean forward until his forehead touched mine. I found it oddly comforting and disturbing. He hadn't refused the claim, and if a no-nonsense Pinkerton Man believed my father could have betrayed us in such a way, it might well be true.

Suddenly, I did not want to find my father.

FIVE

WILLA

"Welcome to the Harvey House!"

The cheerful greeting didn't affect the lady's constipated expression. As a one-woman welcoming committee, she looked part prison warden and part Queen Bee. She stood tall and dominated the lobby of the Kansas City Harvey House.

I gulped, trying to remember why I'd thought being a Harvey Girl was a good idea.

"I'm Mrs. Agnes Q. Downs, your Harvey House dorm mother," the stern lady said. She squinted. "Do I frighten you?"

Clearing my throat, I blinked, thinking fast. The last thing I wanted to do was offend her, but she already seemed offended by my arrival. I'd known women with similar dispositions. We would be at odds unless I distracted her with wit and charm—or just confused her to the point of frustration. It had worked for me once, albeit by accident. "Actually, ma'am, I'm curious as to your middle name. What does Q stand for? It is so rare a letter for a lady that I am assured to be enthralled."

"Don't be clever with me, child."

"I knew a Quinlan," I said as if she'd not reprimanded me. "She was quite a character, but I don't believe it had anything to do with her name. What do you think?"

Mrs. Downs stared at me, the wheels turning. I believe I'd nudged a cog loose. One could almost hear it clanking around in her head. The distress only lasted a moment. She scrunched a thin nose at me which nearly dislodged the wire-framed glasses perched at its end, defying gravity. I seriously doubted they helped her vision, sitting so far away from her peepers.

"You will be given a uniform and assigned a mentor," Mrs Downs said, clearly deciding I wasn't worth a battle.

I took the win. "Will my training start today?"

"The girls work in pairs," Mrs. Downs said. "You will take your cues from a seasoned partner. Didn't you read the handbook?"

The handbook was buried in my suitcase. I would have dragged it out on the train for a quick read, but the trip took several turns that left no time. How could I admit as much to the she-wolf? Instead, I directed the conversation toward the information I needed to find my father. Despite what I'd learned about his possible secret life, I felt compelled to locate him for my mother's sake.

"When will I have a moment to venture into town?" I asked.

Mrs. Downs scoffed. "Whatever for?" Her critical eye sliced across my frame. "At least you're thin. Fitting your uniform won't require alterations. You'll be assigned a room, where you will change and be ready for the next service." She glanced at a gold chatelaine that held a watch at her waist. Tilting the clock face upward, she clucked her tongue. "You have little time to dawdle."

With no chance to question or complain, I was given a uniform and introduced to my mentor, a petite girl named Shirley Ott. Her tired eyes barely held my gaze. The distracted, soul-sapped expression was also reflected in the handful of Harvey Girls I'd seen rushing around.

"We've lost three girls this week," she complained. "They come with grand ideas and let the first dashing stranger whisk them away into marriage."

"Dashing strangers will do that to a girl," I joked.

"Dating the customers is forbidden. And no flirting. All we offer is good food and elegance. Nothing else." She gave me a severe glance. It was the first good view I got of her face. "Is that why you've come, as well? Looking for a rich husband?"

I hadn't planned to tell anyone why I'd journeyed to Kansas City, but opportunities could not be overlooked. "I've come to find my father."

She snarled. "How are you going to do that?"

"I have an address of a residence in town," I said, "and plan to go there and inquire after him."

She snorted. "You don't get time to go into town."

"Why ever not?"

"You are here to work, girly," she said, shaking her head and writing me off. "You'll work. You'll sleep. That will take up all your time."

"I don't need to sleep," I said, wondering if it was safe to journey out at night.

She must have guessed my thoughts. "You have no time to leave this building; if you do, you'll be out of a job. We have a curfew. Do you understand?"

I nodded, but it didn't stop Shirley from muttering under her breath. She got me fitted with the proper clothes and showed me to a shared room on the second floor of the restaurant. It was at the end of a long, narrow hallway. The floorboards creaked, and I didn't see how I could sneak out silently.

"Ten minutes! You hear?" Shirley asked liked she had to repeat it. "You have ten minutes to change and get yourself downstairs." She slammed the door as she left.

"Thank you," I called after her. As a mentor, she could be worse, but not by much.

Standing in the middle of the utilitarian room, I took in the sparse furniture and white walls. My roommate was elsewhere, thankfully, as the space would feel crowded with more than one person. I frowned at the two twin beds, one table with a washbasin, and a solitary window. It looked out over the tracks, making me wonder how late the trains ran.

I laid the uniform on a bed, unsure if I could change into it in ten minutes without wrinkling the perfectly starched material. The uniform consisted of a modest black dress with a high collar and a crisp white apron overlay. It came with a matching white linen strip. I gathered it was for my hair, not that I fancied my ability to tie it into a presentable bow.

I'd seen pictures of Harvey Girls and knew the outfits helped set a standard of fine dining. Even gentlemen passengers were required to wear coats, and every Harvey House was stocked with a supply to loan out. No one was turned away for their attire. The dress code aligned with the whole Harvey House experience—table cloths, china place settings, and sizzling streak dinners served during the short train stops.

If I did something that made a train passenger late to get back on the train...? I didn't want to think about such a mistake. The Kansas City Harvey House had been around for so long that it would survive me.

As I hurried to change, I whispered a quick prayer that my appearance would be as perfectly crisp by the end of the day as it was starting. I took an extra second to rake a comb through my hair. It hung to my shoulders with a gentle wave. The tawny color made the white bow stand out. Miracle of miracles, I'd done a pretty good job tying it. With a silent prayer that I'd survive the coming ordeal, I joined fifteen other Harvey Girls heading downstairs.

We crammed into the hallway between the kitchen and the dining room. I ended up closer to the kitchen. The proximity made my stomach rumble. The air teased the senses with juicy steak drippings and fried butter for the extra-crispy hash browns.

A bell sounded. I'd learn later it was an alert we received minutes before a train arrived. It started the clock on our service, which usually ran for twenty minutes, serving our guests one of the finest meals West of the Mississippi River.

Shirley yanked on my elbow, and I fell into step behind her as the girls filed toward the dining room. "I talk to the passengers and get their order," she hissed. "I signal you, and you hand me the plates of food. We do not speak."

I nodded, wondering if I'd be close enough to hear the order. She quickly explained we'd communicate with subtle hand signals. Two fingers at the side of her skirt meant the customer wanted the sirloin and crispy hash browns. Three fingers the fish and potatoes *Francaise*. Four fingers the pork. If any of her fingers were bent, we had a *howler*, and the manager should have been called. Luckily, it was a short menu, and Shirley took care of the drinks and any substitutions.

The next twenty minutes were a blur. I pasted on a smile and didn't take my eyes off Shirley's fingers. She shook me off a few times, having to tap her fingers against her dress to signal I'd brought the wrong plate. It only took a second to get the right one, but her withering stare put me in my place. Our train guests, however, never noticed. She was able to keep up a polite conversation with the men and reprimand me at the same time.

I was ready to slink up to my tiny room and collapse, but the bell rang again. We'd have three more trains before the day ended. When I finally returned to my room, I learned I'd have it to myself. Another new girl had missed her train and would arrive tomorrow.

"You're lucky," Shirley grumbled. "Use the free bed for your uniform. Get it ready before you sleep. There will be no time in the morning."

"When is the first train?" I asked.

"I'll wake you," she smirked.

The promise gave me a chill. It sounded like waking up the new recruits was a mentor perk. I steeled myself for a trumpet blast in the ear.

Alone in my room, I felt left out. All the other girls had quickly headed to bed, chatting with their roommates. None of them wanted to talk to me. I gathered that it had been a long day after a string of long days. They didn't seem to have the energy for anyone new unless I proved I'd stay for the full six-month contract. I worried I'd be too exhausted tomorrow if I didn't sneak out tonight.

Checking the window, the sun had an hour or so left before it set. I dared to head downstairs and exit to the street. Certainly, I'd find someone outside and ask for directions to my father's house. I clutched the address card in my hand. If this was my only chance, I'd make the most of it. And if Mrs. Agnes Q. Downs popped up and stopped me...? I didn't dare not think of the outcome.

"One disaster at a time," I whispered.

Heading out, I decided to walk like I owned the world and knew where I was going. I'm unsure if my attitude would have worked because I did not cross anyone's path within the Harvey House. I assumed they were all too tired to care about anyone sneaking out. I hoped returning was as simple.

Once on the main street of Kansas City, I asked a man for directions. He looked me up and down but pointed the way. I was close to the address, which left me feeling like the house might have been chosen for the proximity to the train. I quickly walked the three blocks, finding most residents at home. Noises floated to me of children playing in backyards, mothers cleaning up after dinner, and fathers enjoying a pipe on their front porch.

Then I saw it... the house. My heart skipped a beat. It wasn't as grand as our home in New York, but it would do. The red brick was covered in ivy that framed the iron railing along the wrap-around porch. It spoke of lemonade and lazy summers. The two stories were topped by an attic space with dormer windows, their bays hollow abscesses, like dark eyes looking outward. They hid secrets.

I would have patted myself on the back, but locating the home left me cold. Not a single light shone within, and I could not believe I'd found it only to discover it empty.

"This will not do," I muttered, quickly going up the front steps to peer in the window. No sound nor light could be seen from within, but I noticed the window latch was undone.

It really didn't take me long to make the decision to enter. After all, if it was my father's home, wouldn't I have every right to climb in the window like a common thief?

Pushing up the window pane, I struggled to enter. My dress, which I'd changed, trapped my legs. Unless I hiked up the skirt, my progress would be stalled, and standing on the porch felt like being on a stage. I expected someone to spot me and shout: "Intruder!"

Without care for any damage I might cause, I flopped onto my belly and wiggled through the window. However, I misjudged the entry. A low bookcase was set under the window. My entrance knocked over a bronze statue and a stack of books as I slid right over its top and fell to the floor.

"Willa Abbot!"

The voice cried out my name from the street—a familiar voice that made me cringe.

SIX

FINN

I hid in the shadows.

For some reason, watching the Kansas City Harvey House felt different than the million other times I'd tracked and patiently waited to catch a suspect. Of course, Willa Abbot was the farthest thing from a criminal evading capture. Still, she exhibited all the same characteristics.

Cagey, clever, and desperate enough to do the unexpected, I'd have to approach her with caution. I considered my options. The direct approach is usually best, but it could not be employed. It's a luxury that wouldn't work on Willa. More care was needed. Shadowing her every move and swooping in if danger threatened was more to my liking.

After finding her upset on the train, I worried if I was the man for the job. It pained me to see her so, yet the steel in the woman gave me pause. I'd found her in distress, but an inner strength had shown through. What would be a weakness in a man only added to her strength. She would not falter. Nothing, it appeared, would alter her course. Even news of her father's infidelity. I barely noted a moment's doubt.

Frankly, I cursed the man—Cornelius Abbot.

What I knew of Willa's father only added to my concern. She did not deserve to be more parent than daughter. Yet, she would not welcome my instincts. I could only approach with facts. Thus, upon arriving in Kansas City, I sent two telegrams to New York. Loyal colleagues would dig into the elder Abbot's activities. It could take several days until I heard back. Until then, I'd shadow Willa.

Not that I expected much movement. The Harvey House would consume her time. Thus, waiting ticked off the minutes of my day leading into the evening and a one-way debate over how long to linger in the dark. The setting sun stretched across the street, casting shadows big enough to hide my sturdy form.

Knowing the girl would break any house rule, I doubted she'd do so on her first night. Still... she was a surprise wrapped up in the sweetest package. I would not underestimate her. Thus, when the Harvey House back door opened, and a slight figure exited, I followed.

A golden ray caught an escaped wisp of hair, and I knew it was her. Willa did not disappoint. Her audacity rivaled all reason. I had to admire such singleminded focus, even if it tore my heart in two. She'd put herself in danger to find her father; breaking the Harvey House rules and subjecting herself to the denizens of the night—and I couldn't be more impressed.

Dang this woman!

We crossed into a residential neighborhood. I found it rather odd that she walked as if she owned the block. No dainty miss, no sir! Her stride was long, arms relaxed and chin up, like a magnificent horse given the lead.

I took care to keep her in sight without her knowledge. While I was trained in such maneuvers, it chilled my soul that anyone could sneak up unnoticed. She had minimal awareness of her surroundings. I'd have to train her better.

Well... scolding a foolhardy nature might be more needed, yet I could do nothing to hold her down. Such a true spirit needed skills to be safe and successful. I silently added Pinkerton training to the list of things I wished to share with Willa... should I be lucky enough to get the chance.

Hiding behind a tree, I watched her stop at a residence. Dark windows. Cold exterior. It was the loneliest residence on the block. Yet, without hesitation, Willa went up the front steps. Before I could fathom her intention, she pushed open a window. The nerve startled me, but I had only a moment to worry when she climbed over the sill and fell inside.

My heart stopped beating!

WILLA

"Willa Abbot!"

A familiar male voice shouted my name.

Sprawled on the hardwood floor, I got to my knees and peered out the open window—the one I'd just fallen through while breaking into my father's secret second home.

"Willa Abbot," Finn Morgan repeated, quickly coming up the front steps. "Are you injured?"

I blinked, and it had nothing to do with the fading daylight. Of all the people to find me in such a position, it had to be him. The Pinkerton Man frowned, reminding me of the look I'd received after coming to his aid on the train. He'd gotten himself into a tight spot, having cornered a pickpocket. While I'm sure he had the talent to escape any trouble, I had helped with a minor distraction.

He should have thanked me, but Mr. Morgan had not been pleased. The man muttered some nonsense about putting myself in harm's way. When he'd tracked me down afterward, his demeanor held reproof. Upon our arrival in Kansas City, he'd been busy transferring custody of the thief to a local law enforcement officer, and I quickly fled to the Harvey House—only steps away on the train platform. Not another word had passed between us. I'd assumed that I'd seen the last of Finn Morgan.

"Sir, you startled me, and while I might have fumbled my step, I cannot dismiss your interference." I brushed at the front of my skirt, able to see where my dress had dusted off the bookcase on my way inside. No one was taking care of the place.

Finn stared at me, bending to see better inside the window.

"You take no ownership of my tumble?" I cocked my head to one side, expecting an apology.

He smirked. "My pardon, Miss; however, we must account for your climbing skills. I warrant you're rusty when it comes to breaking and entering."

"No breaking was committed, sir." I felt my cheeks flush despite my innocence. "The window was not locked."

"I see. There is still the matter of your midnight outing, is there not?" he asked.

Pointing at the sky, I indicated the setting sun. "Far from midnight."

"Yet, rumor has it that Harvey Girls disappear at sunset. They are locked up." He chuckled to himself. "Have you not broken out?"

His use of breaking in and out was clever, but I'd never admit it. "You are wasting my daylight," I admonished him. "Either come in or go away."

In the fading light, I had the distinct feeling he found my situation humorous or utterly sad. Whichever, I wasn't to know. He climbed in the window, and I turned away to spot a family photograph on the fireplace mantel. The sight of Mother's smiling face caused me a moment, but I had none to spare. The tintype was all the confirmation I needed that father had strayed. I vowed to find out how far and how badly.

"My father is a firm believer in a gentleman's office," I told Finn as I went in search of one.

Finn lit a lantern, joining me down the hallway. It was central to the home. Several rooms branched off it, most sparsely decorated except for the office.

The large room took my breath away. It displayed a grand style, from the crown molding to the rich carpets. Bookcases lined the walls, stuffed to capacity with leather-bound books. I saw one title on Roman Treasures and knew such a topic would interest my father. I went to the desk. The top was orderly enough, so I opened drawers, peering at the paperwork for a clue.

Finn brought the lantern over. Its flame flickered from the movement but helped me read the papers. Most of it seemed like useless correspondence. A credenza behind the desk earned my interest. On top of it sat a small rack holding three pipes. Sadly, they were ones I recognized. I sat in the desk chair, dejected.

"I take it this is your father's house," Finn said, sounding sympathetic.

"Indeed," I answered, fingering one of the pipes. "I am flummoxed."

He sighed. "Don't rush to judgment. While present appearances look bad, more facts could improve your opinion."

While I wanted to take his words to heart, my father still had much to account for. Instead of agreeing with Finn, I turned back to the desk and opened another drawer, frowning. He came around to look inside. It was empty.

"What did you expect to find?" He teased.

"A clue."

He held up the lantern and took in the full scope of the room. It was packed with books, rolled-up graphs, and squirreled-away papers. The space required broad daylight for a full inspection. The very thought made me weak. My enthusiasm for such a chore was low until Fin's lantern illuminated a map on the wall.

"Stop!" I gasped.

I jumped up, grabbed Finn's forearm, and guided the lantern toward the far wall. On it was a map that appeared to be the local area. Small pinned flags marked two spots. "What are we looking at?" he asked.

My heart sank because the map was the worst kind of proof. "Buried treasure," I sighed, having seen such a map before. Father had several over the years. They never led him to the riches, only heartache.

"Your father is a treasure hunter?" The tone of Finn's voice mirrored my disappointment.

"Whatever could he be after this time?" I wondered out loud.

Finn studied the map. "I know something of the local history," he said. "There are stories of Spanish gold. Something about burying it before being massacred by Indians."

I sighed. "How far back was this massacre?"

"It had to be in the 1770's, if I were to guess." Finn held the lantern closer to the map. "Two spots are marked, but they are well outside of town. One is perhaps an hour away, and the other is half the distance."

Missing gold caused by a deadly clash gave me chills. No good could come from it. I did not believe in ghosts, but such a tragic event could not lead to profit. The grime circumstances would taint the whole endeavor.

The map was pinned to the wall. I took it down.

"And what will you do with that, may I ask?" Finn sounded disapproving.

"You know what I'm going to do," I said, tucking the rolled-up map under my arm.

"You think it will lead to your father?"

A host of new complications swirled in my head. "Walk me back to the Harvey House?"

He grunted, snuffed out the lantern, and headed for the front door.

I cleared my throat. "We didn't come in that way."

Finn probably glared at me, but it was getting too dark to tell.

"Any ideas how I can sneak back into the Harvey House without anyone hearing me?" I asked, watching as he exited over the bookcase to join me on the front porch.

He pulled the window shut, stalling an answer but then leaned close to my face. "You're on your own, sweetheart." He winked.

His scent was rather intoxicating—a pleasant mix of leather and oranges. The musky leather was a subtle undertone, dominated by the fruit, which must have been a recent snack. Struggling to focus, I expected him to break away and head to another part of town, but Finn fell into step beside me.

"Never mind," I muttered. I had a short walk to figure it out, but my mind was anything but focused on the task. "Why are you here?" I abruptly asked. A Pinkerton Man certainly had better things to do unless he saw some criminal wrongdoing in my father's actions. "My father has not broken any law."

The statement caused Finn to misstep, but his agility made it barely noticeable. "Outside of lying to his family, your father has done no wrong."

"Yet, a Pinkerton Man has his interest." I accused him.

"No, my interest is not for your father," he said, voice dropping lower. "It is all for you."

I grabbed his arm to stop his forward movement, not because of his shocking admission but because we'd rounded a corner, and the Harvey House came into view. On the second floor, a light shone that should be off. I knew it to be at the top of the stairs. Someone was up, and it would be impossible to pass without a squeaky floorboard giving me away.

He looked at my hand first but then up at the window. "Oh, darn, you are in a pickle."

Seven

Willa

"It's indecent!"

Looking up at the second-floor window to my Harvey House room, I rejected Finn Morgan's suggestion. He wanted to hoist me up so I could crawl through without anyone noticing.

"You already climbed in one window tonight," Finn reminded. "I see no difference. Your reasoning is not immediately obvious, Willa."

The moon shone down on us, lighting the train platform enough so we wouldn't fall off and onto the train tracks. Not that it would put us in danger, except for the fall. No trains would come through at this late hour. I glanced up at my window, knowing it wasn't locked but having no wish for Finn Morgan to manhandle me with a boost to reach the ledge.

"That window was on the main floor," I pointed out. "I'd thank you not to recall the adventure. We should not speak of it again."

He nodded, crossing a finger over his heart. I could feel his smirk but didn't see it. A cloud briefly blocked the moon.

"You asked for my help, and now, once given, you ignore it. Very well, how will you get inside without notice?" he asked.

"I won't." With a little huff of derision, I marched back toward the street and headed for the street-side entrance to the Harvey House—the employee entrance.

"Nice crossing your path, Miss Willa Abbot, as we may not meet again." Finn stopped walking and waited next to the street.

I had plenty to say to the Pinkerton Man, as he'd done me a service: helping at my father's house. Yet, he'd teased me one too many times, and the insinuation that we'd never meet again due to my error struck me all wrong. My mouth stayed shut since I didn't have a kind word to say. Besides, I had far harsher thoughts for myself. I had indeed gotten myself into a pickle, as Finn had claimed, but adding another pickle to my plate made no sense.

Tucking the rolled-up map into my skirt—no sense having to explain that, too—I opened the Harvey House door and hoped for the best. Not that I didn't take care, mind you. My footsteps were as soft as a kitten, with a prayer to the Guardian Angel of Sneaky Sneaks that the floorboards would be quiet. I also added a wish that any sound I created was lost amongst the snoring. Believe me, ladies snore. Not that I'd ever tell a Harvey Girl she carried on like a lumberjack! I'd keep that to myself.

Halfway down the hallway, thinking the angels were cushioning every step I took, my luck ran out. A creak reverberated in the narrow passage, sounding louder than fingers on a blackboard. The door at the top of the stairs—the dorm mother's door—instantly opened.

I spun around, caught sneaking back to my room.

Plato believed that necessity was the mother of invention, and somewhere along the way, it became a Proverb. That Proverb popped into my panicked brain. With nary a heartbeat, I rubbed my eyes and gawked at Mrs. Agnes Q. Downs.

"Am I late or early?" I asked as if my voice had been dipped in slumber.

"It's nighttime, young lady." The Matron frowned. "Why are you dressed?"

I let my eyes flutter at half-mast. "Oh, good," I mumbled. "Haven't missed my train."

Mrs. Downs came right up to me and poked me in the arm.

Swaying away from her, I sighed and shut my eyes, head drooping forward. I stopped short of snoring, but I sucked in a ragged breath, sighing again. She'd either think I was drunk—not my intention—or sleepwalking.

Mrs. Downs took me gently by the shoulders and turned me around. "There, there, girlie. No train today. Just back to bed with you."

With more care than I'd ever expect from the she-bear, she guided me back to my bed. At her whispered suggestion, I sat, and she coaxed me to lie down. I almost giggled with glee. Muttering a curse, Mrs. Downs pulled a comforter over me, letting me stay in my street clothes.

"Of all the worrisome nonsense," she mumbled, heading back into the hall.

I was of half a mind to blow her a kiss. Who knew she was an old softie?

Peeking over the comforter, I could see my door was shut, and my only companion was a guilty conscience. With a tug at my waistband, I pulled the treasure map out of my skirt. It had a new crease. Drats and rats! It couldn't be helped, so I slid it under the mattress, hoping it would also press out the damage. Then, I plopped back on the bed, exhausted.

The morning sun woke me before Mrs. Downs got a chance. I sat up, startled by a murky dream and momentarily confused about why I was dressed. It took a second to remember my charade. A flush heated my cheeks. It wasn't my nature to play-act in such a way, but I had to do it for Mother. I couldn't go back to her just yet, not without more information.

I laid down again, wondering if I'd have to apologize to Mrs. Downs. I failed to tell her I was a sleepwalker. Not that I'd ever done so in my life, but now I'd be labeled one in the Matron's records. That practically made it true, and I'd have to own it.

"It rarely happens," I practiced the lie. It rang false.

Oh my, the Harvey House matron would see right through me! Ruin waited down that path, so I decided to avoid it as long as possible. After all, would a sleepwalker even remember the faux pas? Probably not. Thus, I'd leave it to Mrs. Downs to bring up the incident before I launched into an awkward lie.

I moaned and covered my face with both hands. A sinking feeling settled in my stomach. I'd be telling a library full of lies before this adventure ended. Luckily, life in the Harvey House didn't allow time for regrets.

A knock and a gruff: "You awake?" came from the other side of my door. It must have been my wake-up call and not from Mrs. Downs. The unfriendly voice sounded like my mentor, Shirley. I grunted in the affirmative, and before I knew it, I was in my perfectly crisp uniform, waiting with the other Harvey Girls as the first train arrived at the station.

During one of our breaks between trains—we had three throughout the day—I rushed back to my room. Mrs. Downs caught my eye as I left the dining room. She gave me a little nod, checking up on me, I guessed. I stopped for a quick curtsey—something a city girl would never do, not any in my acquaintance—but Mrs. Downs rewarded me with a thin smile. It stretched her lips to the breaking point.

She'd taken last night's disturbance well. I imagined that the first time would be forgotten, but a second would be Hell. I vowed to plan my re-entry plans as much as my exit plans in the future.

Slipping into my room, I pulled out the map and studied the terrain. Short of traveling to the two marked spots, I desperately hoped to find another option. Any little clue that would lead me to my father.

My bedroom door banged open, and I gasped, unable to hide the treasure map.

A girl about my age entered, face rosy, hair wild, and arms full of luggage. She dropped the bags on the floor. "Oh, excuse me, I must have startled you!" The girl touched her blonde bun, tucking in a loose strand. "I'm your new roommate. Call me Dolores, no call me Dori, Dori Hilbert, and please explain why everyone here is so cross. It hardly bodes well. I have no idea what I've gotten myself into, although I'm quite intrigued by your treasure map."

She walked over, tapping a finger against her lips.

"It's just a map," I said, wondering how I'd get out of this one.

"If you say so," Dori said, "you might be mistaken. See this little mark?" Leaning forward, she tapped a spot in the bottom left corner. "It's a cartographer's mark. Sort of a secret, but not so secret symbol."

Scrunching up my nose to see it better, I acknowledged the symbol. It looked like an ornamental design. Something mapmakers add to show off their artistic talents. Could it actually mean more?

"Oh my, oh my," Dori muttered. "This is much more than a treasure map. It's THE treasure map!"

She playfully punched me in the arm, like we were the oldest friends. However, two things were running through my mind: *Who is this girl, and how do I get rid of her?*

EIGHT

DORI - 1891, AGE 18
LOYAL, BOOKISH, WINSOME.

Drat! I've done it again!

All my hopes were dashed in an instant. *Wonderful, Dori*, I silently grumbled to myself. Hadn't even been at the Harvey House for an hour, and I'd alienated my only friend. Well... my almost friend. Err... someone I hoped would be my bestest friend in the whole world? At the very least, a pleasant girl who wouldn't smother me in my sleep.

Alas, I didn't even know my roommate's name, and she already hated me. I couldn't help saying what I had about the treasure map because I'd seen one before. Several. Old ones and the one my roommate had was quite old.

"I'm sorry if I spoke out of turn," I said, trying to explain myself, "but you have a treasure map whether you like it or not." With a broad smile, I nodded emphatically. "You should like it. While I've seen four in my short life, they are rare."

The girl blinked as if she didn't understand.

"You can trust me," I said, sticking out my hands to show my fingers were stained with blotches of black ink. "I draw maps. A hobby, if you will, though Pa told me to keep that fact to myself. They don't teach girls the skill, but no one could stop me. I'm naturally gifted."

My smile grew with pride. A big horsey smile, my Pa called it. We always giggled over that one. I tried to smile a little less, but I couldn't help it. Of all the things I was good at, my abilities with maps pleased me to no end. My other minimal skills included piano, needlepoint, cooking, mathematics, French, calligraphy, basket weaving, flower pressing, cartography, and spotting constellations. Being so stunted in my education was a burden, but I'd learned most of my knowledge by eavesdropping.

As you will note, I do not claim eavesdropping as a skill. It's a curse.

"Stop, please stop," my roommate gasped with a little moan. Her auburn hair shimmered. I almost commented on it, but pretty girls usually hated such notice.

Instead, I snapped my attention back to her stunned expression. "I'm sorry to cause you distress," I said, "but what's your name?"

"Willa Abbot."

My roommate blinked rapidly as if she needed a little more sleep. The bags under her eyes were another clue that she'd had a bad night. I looked around the room, wondering which bed was hers. They were both made and looked so neat, I was impressed. My roommate Willa was exceptionally tidy unless she'd slept on top of the sheets. I was only minimally tidy; thus, I vowed to watch and learn.

I said as much, causing Willa to groan. If the pain came from her body or some adverse reaction to me, I could not tell. Who wouldn't like me? And I had to assume we held the same desire... having both taken the challenge of becoming a Harvey Girl.

"Whatever you do," Willa said, giving me a leveled, intense stare, "don't tell anyone about the map. Do you understand?"

I nodded.

Willa appeared satisfied.

"But," I had to add, "there is one thing you must know about your treasure map."

Her head jerked in my direction. "Stop calling it that."

"What should I call it?" My mind went blank. It made no sense to call a thing anything other than what it was.

"In my experience, a treasure map is a treasure map... unless it's something more." I clapped my hands together, peering closer at the design along the edge of the map.

"Just stop calling it that, and stop looking at it." Willa rolled up the map.

The protective approach made sense when it came to treasure, but the true riches were in the map itself. It was a thing of beauty that had been created by a talented cartographer who most surely was long dead. And that fact gave me a delicious thrill!

WILLA

"Oooh, your treasure map is marvelous!"

My new roommate, the overeager, bright-eyed Dori Hilbert, pointed toward the map I'd found in my father's secret second home—now hidden under my mattress. She didn't seem to understand that I wanted to keep it private.

"Not another word," I admonished her.

Dori stepped back, finally noticing my face. I assumed it looked as mortified as I felt. It had to be red. I could feel the heat. The last thing I needed was a chatterbox for a roommate. Especially since I was so careless as to expose my biggest, darkest secret—the treasure map. "It's an ordinary map," I said, "and no one needs to know about it. Understand?"

The girl blinked quickly; I couldn't tell if my forceful words had elicited tears or if she needed a moment to compose herself. A pang of guilt hit me as Dori went from starry-eyed newcomer to reprimanded roommate. I'd done that, and it didn't feel good. The poor girl seemed to have lost her ability to talk, although that might serve her well at the Harvey House. Still, I felt like the worst lug head.

A bell sounded. Hurried footsteps echoed in the hallway, and I knew we had less than ten minutes to return to the dining room and put on our best smiles. It was our first gift to the train passengers—a genuine welcoming greeting. I might have to force mine this time.

Dori's head jerked to the door. "What's that?"

"It's our cue to head downstairs," I said, pointing at the uniform she'd dropped with her luggage. "Put that on and come down unless Mrs. Downs told you otherwise."

Perplexed, Dori shrugged one shoulder. "No one has told me anything."

I moved toward the door, knowing Dori could be late on her first day, but I could not. "Change and come down to the dining room. You know where that is, I take it?"

She nodded yes.

"Change and come down." I sighed, wondering how many times I'd have to repeat myself.

Dori looked like lightning had struck her, movements jerky and steam practically escaping from the top of her head. Well... I imagined the steam, but it wasn't a stretch.

"And don't touch my map!" I hissed, heading into the hall and hoping she'd regain her composure. Leaving her and the map in the same room felt all kinds of wrong, but being late would be worse.

I was the last to arrive downstairs, but I slid into my spot before the first train passenger rushed into the dining room. Mrs. Downs raised an eyebrow at me, and I gave her a quick nod, hoping she'd take it as confirmation that I was ready to serve. She had to know about Dori's arrival and probably expected me to help her acclimate.

Focusing on Shirley's hand signals, I moved with grace and speed, flawlessly delivering each dish. She winked at me, which I took as high praise. Shirley steered clear of compliments and saved all her positivity for the passengers. I accepted her demeanor amicably, despite an inquisitive nature that made me wonder if her stoic facade hid a heartache. Something had surely sapped away her emotions. However, that mystery would have to wait.

When I finally returned to my room, it was with some trepidation. I hadn't a moment to think about what I could or should say to Dori. While I had come down on her rather hard, it felt necessary in the moment. She'd startled me with her arrival, keen eyes, and constant talking. I still had no idea how she had gleaned the nature of my map.

Part of me wanted to share my quest. She could be helpful. She could also rat me out to Mrs. Downs. I had no delusions about how our watchdog matron would react to the map—with a reprimand and a dismissal! While I'd discovered a soft side, the dragon lady had a job to do, and treasure hunting would be frowned upon. It was rather unseemly for the high standards of a Harvey Girl. Well... it would not be a welcome endeavor for anyone in polite society. It was the very reason I'd kept my journey a secret from Mother.

A tepid knock tapped at the bedroom door. Before I could move, it opened, and Dori poked her head inside. "It's me," she said, as cheerful as ever.

I wondered if even a full day in the dining room would dampen her sparkle. She had an indomitable spirit. One I admired.

"You don't have to knock," I said, motioning for her to enter.

"I didn't want to startle you twice in one day." She came in and shut the door behind her. With a glance at the knob, she frowned. "No lock. You might want to prop a chair under the knob the next time you need to study your M-A-P." She winked knowingly.

The girl had a point, although spelling out the thing she shouldn't talk about was puzzling. Did she think we were hiding it from a child?

"I apologize," I said, not really wanting to list my errors. "I reacted badly, and you took it with grace."

Dori clucked her tongue. "Never you mind. I'm far too nosey. Pa chastises me often on the point. It's you that should forgive me. Please be assured, I shall take the knowledge of your... item—and what it might or might not be—to my grave." She crossed a finger back and forth over her heart, then kissed it.

While I appreciated the gesture, it was a tad dramatic. I sighed. "You cannot unsee what you have seen. While we are alone together, you may speak freely."

Plopping onto the edge of her bed, Dori made the springs groan with the sudden weight. "Oh! I would certainly aid you in any way I may in the most discreet manner. It would be my pleasure!"

Dori reminded me of a little kid with a new toy. Or a puppy who discovered its tail.

"How do you know so much about maps?" I would possibly regret it later, but I decided to use Dori's knowledge to help plot my next move.

"We have a long line of professors in my family," Dori admitted.

She did not elaborate. I stared at her for a moment, curious that once asked a direct question, she clammed up.

"Oh!" Dori finally got my meaning. "Silly me. My family are history professors, and cartography is vital for historians. I have personally been drawn to bygone maps. They are works of art, don't you know? It piqued my interest even more when I learned how the artistic flourishes disguise hidden information. Isn't history interesting?"

I nodded. Pulling the map from under my mattress, I flattened it on my bed. "Very interesting," I said. "Even more remarkable if you can point out the ones you see on my map."

Dori came over to the bed and knelt down. She studied the map's designs. After a moment, she pointed at each corner in turn. They all contained a detailed design of flourishes, foliage, and forest animals. "Each area holds a clue to find another part of the map."

"Another part?" I shook my head. The map was in perfect condition. No part of it appeared to be missing.

"I believe there are four overlays," Dori said. "Find the missing pieces, lay them over your map, and they will reveal directions to the treasure."

The girl was brilliant! Indeed, an angel was sent here to help me. At the very least, I had Fred Harvey to thank. His high standards brought in the most clever girls. Dori had proved she'd been taught well and encouraged in ways most women were not. It struck me that she was worthy of being a professor if allowed. She should have been at university, studying her beloved history. Instead, her brilliance would only benefit me.

Dumbfounded by the map's complexity, I sat back on my heels. Crouching to study it made my thighs ache, and hearing that I was missing four parts gave me a headache. It was the worst news, meaning my father did not possess the whole map. Was he trying to find the missing pieces? According to Dori, he could not find the treasure without the overlays.

"How do you know all this?" I asked, hoping she was guessing and had jumped to conclusions.

She tapped an engraving that arched over the top of the map. "It's Latin and says you need four overlays."

I sighed. Latin was not a skill I'd mastered. "Dori, I am beholding to you."

A soft pitter-patter echoed from the window. We both looked over at it. The sound could have been rain against the window pane; however, the sky looked clear. Dori went to the window and peeked out.

"Oh, my!" she gasped.

"What is it?" I asked.

Dori turned to me with a broad smile. "It is a most handsome gentleman."

Groaning, I went to the window and opened it. Sticking my head out, I frowned at the man. "Finn Morgan, this is most familiar."

The Pinkerton Man smiled up at me. "I take it you have not been sent home."

I shushed him. "Please, take yourself away, sir; this is not befitting a lady's honor."

"When can I call on you?" he asked with a smirk. "I have news."

Drat the scoundrel! He knew precisely how to weasel his way into a tete-a-tete, and I almost hated him for it. Almost, because Mother always told me that hate should be reserved for the truly despicable. Finn Morgan was only marginally intolerable.

With a huff and a certainty that I'd regret asking the question, I whispered, "What revelation have you brought to my door?"

NINE

FINN

"Aren't you cute!"

Another girl joined Willa in the window, full of energy. Her blonde hair was in a bun with bang ringlets, and she had the biggest smile I'd ever seen.

"My roommate—Dori," Willa said without enthusiasm, even though she briefly winked at the girl.

I gave Dori a little wave, and she blushed.

"Your revelation?" Willa prompted, sounding impatient.

Stalling, I knew my news would need some privacy. Several windows faced the train platform. Lights shone from them, and even though train service had stopped for the night—thus leaving the platform relatively private—a prolonged conversation could draw notice.

"I require a moment alone if you will indulge me." I heard my request as I spoke it and worried it sounded like a tête-à-tête. "Your father would not wish his business discussed openly."

Despite the added explanation, the awkwardness lingered, possibly one-sided. Standing below her window, uncertain of the response, my true feelings could not be ignored. They thumped in my chest and twisted my resolve. The foreign sensation crippled my will—and this from a Pinkerton Man? I silently berated myself, having never encountered such a debilitating condition.

I'd certainly avoided female entanglements, and this was why. They did nothing but derail sensible men. Ever since meeting Willa Abbot, I'd made mistakes. The first was being enchanted by her spunk. The second was taking steps to stay in Kansas City when my duty lay farther West. But I'd asked for time off from the Pinkertons, telling myself it was logical. The mystery of Willa's father, Cornelius Abbot, could lead to finding a gang of notorious con men. The Pinkertons would eventually thank me.

It's a good career move, I lied to myself.

Who was I kidding? It was dumb luck. What I hadn't admitted to myself—couldn't accept until now—was I'd use any excuse to stay near Willa.

The truth struck me hard. Something shifted when we met. Imperceptible, at first, but had snuck up fast and could not be ignored. It made me act secretly. I had to protect my heart and aid her in any way possible. Perhaps she would never know what drove me. Presently, I'd rather face an army of maniacs with only one bullet in my gun than bare my soul to the confounding, intoxicating Willa Abbot.

No man would risk such torture. I certainly had not been trained for it. Thus, I shall see this to the end—helping Willa find her father—and then determine if she's left anything of my heart.

WILLA

"I bring difficult news."

Finn Morgan's statement shook me to the core. Staring down at him, I felt weak and had to grab the frame for support. The movement made Dori duck back into the room, and I filled the window, needing a moment. Luckily, my new roommate seemed to understand.

For the briefest of butterfly moments, I had dared to hope the news was good. It seemed otherwise, and suddenly, Finn's unwavering assistance, my Harvey House indoctrination, and even the last splashes of glittering sun dipping behind ragged hills held no enchantment. I could comprehend little else beyond fixing whatever had gone wrong.

"Tell me what you have learned!" I gasped, barely able to contain my heart.

He frowned up at me. "Please, Willa, we must talk privately."

Since it was after hours, no one lingered on the platform with Finn. The train-side of the Harvey House was entirely vacant. It would not see activity until morning. I was about to say no one could overhear when another second-floor window opened. Just ten feet to my left, in the very next room, a girl's head poked out. I'd seen her, yet we hadn't officially been introduced—another Harvey Girl. Her long dark hair swung around her chin, rolled up in rags. The strands bobbed with every turn of her head.

"What's with all the chatter?" Rag-curls asked, pursing her lips together. It was more out of curiosity than reproach. Her roommate squeezed out beside her for a peek but spotted Finn and put a hand over her mouth.

I signaled them to go back inside. They paid me no heed.

"Oooh," Miss Rag-curls cooed, "we've interrupted a beau coming to call. Hey, mister, you scoot along. Harvey Girls sign a contract. She'll lose her whole salary if you take her away from all this."

"You can take me away from all this!" the audacious roommate shouted.

"Please!" I interrupted. "This is none of your concern."

"But it's entertaining!" the roommate giggled. I vaguely recalled her name. Something with a B and as silly sounding as her hiccuping laughter.

"If you must know," I added, "my father is missing, and this man has news of him."

Luckily, my words touched their kind hearts. Rag-curls waved a hand in front of her face, suddenly sad. The roommate, however... Bitty, Bunny, Bluebonnet... sighed the biggest, chest-heaving sigh I'd ever seen.

"What a dear," she sighed, unable to take her eyes off Finn.

"I try my best." Finn's smirk was far too pleased with himself.

I gaped at the Pinkerton Man, deciding he liked the attention. "I beg you," I pleaded with the girls. "I just need a moment, and then he'll be gone."

"Nooooo," the roommate reached out a hand to Finn, far too high for contact. "Let him stay."

"If it's family news," Rag-curls said, "have him come round to the staff door like a proper caller. Mrs. Downs will allow you a brief meeting in our little parlor."

"I'll chaperone!" Rag-curls's roommate waved a hand, giddy. However, the gleam in her eye would have sent any man running. It even had that effect on me.

"I'll chaperone!" Dori insisted, pushing me to the side and poking her head back out our window. "We thank you for your assistance, but that will be all."

The Harvey Girls pouted, disappointed.

"Yes, yes," I interjected, elbowing Dori to go back into the room. "My roommate can chaperone." I smiled at the girls.

They had certainly done me a kindness. Some house rules were less evident than others, especially regarding the little parlor. "If you will." I motioned for Finn to head around to the street. "I'll meet you."

With a tip of his bowler hat, Finn gladly departed amidst the whistles and hoots of my Harvey Girl neighbors.

"Thank you kindly," I waved at the girls, ducking back into the room. I turned to Dori, a finger pointed toward the map. "We can't bring that, but I would certainly appreciate your assistance as a chaperone."

Dori stood straight, a hand to test if her hair was neat enough to meet a caller. "If you introduce me to your handsome caller, it would be my pleasure. I know he's sweet on you; thus, I'd be honored to make his acquaintance."

"He's not sweet on me," I said, banishing the thought. "He's more like a mangy dog that follows you home for kitchen scraps."

Appearing to have difficulty rationalizing my description with her Finn fantasy, Dori tutted for a minute, busying herself with making sure the map was safely under my mattress. "Oh, he does sound like a handful," she said, straightening her skirt. "I'll happily act as a chaperone and make doubly certain he behaves."

"I can handle him, but your presence is most welcome. Now come along and say nothing of the you-know-what." I winked at my mattress. "Although he knows it exists, he has not studied it."

Dori nodded that she understood, pretending to lock her lips. It took only a brief stop at Mrs. Downs's room to get her approval. Not even a bit of side-eye, and we were off to the parlor. I must admit to backing away from her door with a stunned expression. I'd clearly missed some Harvey House perks.

Once we settled in the parlor, Finn greeted us with a sad smile. "The news is not..."

"Good?" Dori interrupted. "Or... not as bad as it could be? Or worth our worry? Or likely to help Willa find her father? Or... dear me, the biggest disaster known to man?!"

The stream of words sped out of Dori like a runaway train. If any were the completion of Finn's news, he was too taken aback to admit it. I shuddered and gently put a hand on her arm. "Please, take a seat," I begged Dori. She meant well, but I carried enough worry without help.

As Dori sunk to a brocade settee, I faced Finn. "How bad is it?"

"Your father's business partner was found... dead." Finn held his hat in his hands. "At your father's house."

"The house we went to yesterday?" I turned away from him, unable to picture the scene. "Was it the man from the train?"

"Yes," Finn said, "He broke into your father's house. I've been to the scene, and the home is in disarray. Possibly ransacked. There was evidence of a struggle. It must have happened after our visit."

"Your father has a house in town?" Dori piped up.

Finn and I looked at her, then back at each other. "What of my father?"

"No sign," Finn said. "He is wanted..."

"For murder?" Dori interrupted.

"Please, Dori dear, silence is much appreciated," I whispered to her, but the question she posed had also popped into my mind.

Dori slumped on the settee.

"At the moment, your father is only wanted for questioning." Finn rubbed his chin. I took it as a clear sign that he had more to tell me but was unsure if he should.

I motioned for Finn, stepping away from Dori and lowering my voice. "If you have more news of my father, please share it. I cannot fathom this turn of events; every detail is salient."

Finn nodded. He struck me as a sensible man, after all. "I have learned that your father was seen in town nine days prior but not since. Nothing points to his return."

It wasn't the worst news. Something could have happened to Father, but I would not borrow trouble. He left the map behind for a reason. Perhaps he sent a man after it, but he was accosted by the disgruntled partner. Father could be waiting for his man's return—with the map. Since I had the map, all their plans would be foiled.

"I can see the wheels turning," Finn said, "and can only imagine the outcome. Shall you expose your machinations?"

I raised a finger, stalling a direct answer. "Is more known of the dead man's—my father's business partner's—identity?"

"His name was Reggie Brown," Finn said. "Had you missed it on the train?"

"Mister Brown's mission was so earnest, he did not share it." Picturing the man in the green-checkered suit, he'd been focused on exposing Father's second home in Kansas City. It seemed to be his only purpose in approaching me. "Had he used me as bait? Did my appearance at Father's house set all this in motion?" With a hand to my heart, I joined Dori on the settee.

She patted my hand, and I realized she'd heard everything but had politely remained silent on the matter. It proved she could be trained from blurting out everything that crossed her mind. Promising.

Finn shifted on his feet, uneasy, as if he expected an enormous explosion from my lips. There would be none of that. I had no time for hysterics.

"Whatever has gone awry, my father is in danger," I stated. "The map I found at his house has hidden clues. They could very well lead to the Spanish gold."

"I thought we weren't going to talk about you know what, hidden under you know where," Dori whispered.

Finn smirked. "Willa knows better than to keep secrets from me."

My eyes found his smug face. "If the map is critical to finding Father and the murderer, then you must know that the map is incomplete. It requires four overlays, which we must find before the treasure can be unearthed. If the treasure exists."

Crossing his arms, Finn considered me. It would not be bragging to say he did so with a look of awe. Something in the vicinity of my heart fluttered, but I paid it no mind. I did, however, need Finn's help.

"On my day off," I said, "I shall visit one of the map's marked spots and see what can be learned. Until then, the map will stay under my protection unless you mean to confiscate it."

I raised my chin.

With a low chuckle, Finn held up both hands. "Far be it for me, Miss Abbot, to interfere with your investigation."

A frown settled over my lips. "Indeed, sir, I expect a Pinkerton Man to swoop in and take charge."

"Happy to dissuade you of the notion," Finn said with a slight bow. "This is not my case nor of any Pinkerton agent. I am at your service until I deem the situation deserves the local authorities. Presently, waving a treasure map around is not the soundest action unless we wish to appear as addle-headed buffoons."

Dori clapped her hands. "We should pack a picnic and head for the foothills."

"The foothills?" Finn's tone sounded doubtful. Whether it was the plan or Dori in general, I could not tell.

"That was the closest spot that I noticed," Dori said.

Backing her up, I chimed in support. "An Elemental wind symbol marks one corner of the map and indicates where we may find an overlay."

"Up high," Dori added, "I should imagine in the most dangerous spot. Maps of this nature would hardly make for an easy discovery, as the item would have to withstand centuries before being found."

Finn's bright eyes flashed, and he gave every indication of wanting to question Dori but thought better of it. He might, in fact, be rethinking our whole plan, but I didn't allow him to back out. Standing, I thrust out my hand to shake his. He took it. His touch was so gentle that I thought he shook on our union reluctantly. When his eyes held mine a bit too long, I wondered if I was reading him right. Was it reluctance or dread? Dear me, what could Finn Morgan dread about me?

"Have no fear," I beamed at him, "no mountain is too high, no peak insurmountable. We shall find the rest of the map if it is the last thing we do!"

Finn pulled his hand out of my grip. "No, it is not the last thing we will do. On the contrary, no one shall die trying. Do you hear me, Willa? We shall take precautions and sound steps. No harm will come to you."

"Or you," I added.

"Or me!" Dori gulped. "My, my, and people say I'm the dramatic one."

TEN

WILLA

"Oh, my pumpkins!"

I gulped for air, hugging the cliffside and trying to calm a racing heart. My bold statement about 'no mountain being too high' mocked me. Regret filled my very soul, fighting valiantly against a numbing fear.

My father's treasure map had led us to the limestone bluffs overlooking the Missouri River that ran through Kansas City. Pitted and weathered, the landscape was dense with vegetation. It jutted precariously in spots, especially those leading to the highest point. We'd spotted a log cabin during our climb but had not encountered another soul. I worried a bit over trespassing, but surely we'd talk our way

out of that particular danger. Taking a nasty fall was far
more likely.

I'd insisted on this journey, putting my new friends'
lives in danger, not to mention my own. However, my
companions showed no sign of concern. Finn, up ahead on
the winding path, kept a steady pace forward. He glanced
back regularly, possibly to see if we were still following or
had regained our sanity, and backtracked to a safe spot.

Chancing a look over my shoulder, I checked on Dori,
bringing up the rear of our group. She smiled back, nary
a care in the world. "We're almost there!" she shouted
encouragement.

Perched as we were between gnarly tree trunks and a slope
leading to a sheer drop, the wind whistled through leaves
and tugged at our clothes. I put a hand to my hair, feeling
the bun had loosened. One tug and it came loose. I quickly
re-tied my hair into a ponytail. It would have to do for now.
The path required all my attention.

Only a big horn sheep could manage the pitch, making
me think animals had worn the trail. It was not meant for
human feet. However, it matched a twisting red line on
my father's map. Dori noticed it immediately, indicating we
had found the right hiking spot.

Hike. I grumbled the word, knowing I only had myself to
blame... well, Father should shoulder a bit of the burden.
All of this was to find him. Not physically, at this point,

but if we located one of the map's overlays, we'd be closer to finding the treasure—and thus Father.

That was my hope. Alas, we were working on a theory. I feared my educated guesses would be dashed at any turn, and we'd have to start from scratch. I did, however, count myself lucky to have two friends willing to go along with my schemes. And, yes, I'd begun to think of Dori and Finn as friends. It was easy with Dori but also entirely natural regarding the Pinkerton Man. He'd proven to be very handy. Like a brother. Well,... not exactly like a family member, but a trusted compatriot who only wanted the best for me.

When it came to family, I was all flustered. The questions I had about Father's treasure hunt were mounting. After all the things I'd learned, it seemed my father had found the map but stopped to search to come home to New York City. Then, he'd suddenly left us to take up the search again? It made no sense. At first, I did not believe he'd departed our home by choice, but my doubts on that front had doubled.

I'd had no time to sort it all out, but the questions lingered. I couldn't avoid them forever. Especially the ones concerning Father's actions. Plus, I fretted over how long I could keep it all from Mother. She'd be mortified, but possibly more over my actions than the man she'd married. Did she know the extent of his duplicity? Should I learn anything if I were to confide in her? A letter would not do. It required a face-to-face conversation, which would not happen anytime soon.

Worrying would have to wait. I needed all my attention to navigate the narrow path. While I wanted to keep my eyes on the horizon or treeline, that would be folly. I had to look down. Had to spot each step since only inches separated my right foot from slipping downward. The limestone had given way in several spots, and trees had uprooted and pitched in awkward angles. Looking down took my breath away, but I had to look.

"This is the highest point!" Finn shouted. He'd reached a natural lookout. The trees were thicker, affording us some safety.

I reached him first, and Dori quickly closed the distance. Her speed made my stomach lurch. "Do take care," I warned her.

Dori smiled back. "There it is!" she pointed at a solid rock formation between a clump of trees. The elements had done their magic, carving a slot over time in the exposed rock. "Is it too high to reach? The overlay would be wrapped in animal skin and oiled to protect it, then shoved into the slot. That's my guess."

She looked between Finn and me as if waiting for one of us to climb up onto the rock for a proper inspection.

"I can help you up," Finn offered. He laced his fingers together and held them low. They presented a step to get me closer to the hidden spot.

I quickly glanced at the slope to our right and decided we were on sturdy ground. I stepped onto Finn's hand, reaching to steady myself against the rocky outcropping. He pushed me high enough to see into the crevice. "It's empty," I moaned.

Carefully bringing me back to his level, Finn's hands went to my waist. I ended up facing him, grasping his broad shoulders. The closeness was like nothing I'd ever experienced, leaving me quite breathless.

"We are too late," I whispered. "The overlay is gone."

Finn tilted his head to the side. I could feel his disappointment, more for me than himself. He'd taken up my adventure, and I owed him for all his help. I wanted to acknowledge as much, but the words failed me. They also seemed to escape him as his eyes held mine in a silent communication that made my toes tingle.

"Do you think your father already found this one?" Dori asked, ever practical and clueless to the moment unfolding with the perplexing Pinkerton Man.

"I should have considered that possibility," I said, realizing that the treasure map would only be left on Father's wall if he no longer needed it. "Do you suppose they've located all the overlays?"

"Very likely," Finn said. "I suppose your father and his partners got here first."

His hands fell away from my waist, eyes to the tiny alcove, perhaps contemplating how many treasure hunters were following the map's clues.

I blinked, shocked that our luck had run out, but I saw something. "What's that?" I nodded my chin up at the space. "Are those symbols?"

We squeezed together to stare at the spot. Indeed, three symbols were etched in the stone at the back of the tiny alcove. Darkened with age, they were barely visible. I squinted. The hieroglyphs were unfamiliar. Dori took out a little notebook and sketched the figures. She was full of valuable skills.

"More clues," Finn said as if it were some kind of curse.

"Father and his partners may have all the overlays." I sighed, closing my eyes against another horrifying thought. "Had Mr. Reggie Brown been killed for the overlays? Could he have possessed them and gone to Father's house for the map?"

Dori put away her sketchbook. "If so, the killer will be after the map next."

Since the treasure map was snuggly hidden under my mattress, I didn't worry about anyone finding it. "No one knows about me."

"Yet," Finn warned. "We'll have to speak with the local authorities now, I'm afraid. They might find a treasure hunt pure folly, but they will have seen many a crime erupt over such shenanigans."

The outing had taken three days to plan. I couldn't believe it had come to nothing. Less than nothing, as I now had to speak with the local constable or sheriff or whatever form of law they had in Kansas City. I was ashamed that I did not know.

"What of the other overlays?" Dori asked. "We can't assume they were found."

"I believe we can, for now." Finn crossed his arms over his chest.

Leaning against a tree, I marveled at the view of Kansas City. The town spread out before us, stretching farther than I had imagined. We'd driven to the bluff by buggy, Finn insisting on renting one. His help had been invaluable. I was about to say as much when the ground shifted under our feet. I looked down, finding my boots sinking with the limestone. Finn and Dori were further back, but the tree—and my feet—were too close to the edge. Birds flew away, alarmed, and a hissing, twisting, crunching of earth rumbled as the ground disappeared under my feet, and I fell, along with a big chunk of the hillside.

I looked up just in time to see Finn's shocked face, and then my stomach lurched as my world shifted downward.

ELEVEN

WILLA

"Willa, run!"

Dori screamed too late.

The limestone cliff broke away under my feet. For a sickening moment, the horizon tilted, and I hung in mid-air. Time stalled, and I expected my life to flash before my eyes. I'd heard such things happen just before a sudden death.

Oh, what a disastrous end to our outing! And I'd been so keen on enjoying a picnic basket with Finn. And Dori, of course.

My despair, however, was cut short when gravity and the logical part of my brain snapped back into play. I wasn't falling. No, indeed. The rocks and sediment cleaved and crashed in a twisted orchestra under my shoes, but I had not disappeared with the rubble. A strong arm gripped my waist.

Finn pulled me close and onto solid ground.

I couldn't speak. Breathing was barely possible. I only sensed the beating of my heart. Or was it his heart? The man's chest was too darn close to tell. A proper lady would not comment, but he bent his head to mine. We lightly touched. Now, I couldn't tell if his lips or his chin had brushed the top of my head. I'm pretty confident it wasn't his nose. That would ruin the moment. It had to be his lips.

Oh my, is it wrong to wonder—in the throws of sheer terror—if Dori had noticed a kiss?

"Of all the daring do," Dori chuckled. "You two put on a magnificent show."

I patted Finn's chest. His solid, solid chest. "Can we go down now?"

"I'm rather afraid to let go of you," he muttered. Panic hung between each word. His concern touched my heart, but this was not the time nor place to lose ourselves. I'm relatively sure Mother would disapprove.

Dori clapped her hands together. "You should carry her down. I dare say her knees are weak."

"No!" I managed, wiggling out of his grasp. "It was almost nothing. The smallest of disasters. Finn's quick action saved the day, but such heroics will not solve the bigger problem."

"Of course, you are correct," Finn said, motioning me to work my way downward through the trees and away from the edge.

"As you wish," Dori said, "but our Mister Finn is a keeper!" She practically skipped down the path, not caring if the cliff crumbled under her feet.

I caught Finn's eye and smiled. "Thank you," I mouthed the words, more than a little chagrin that I needed saving.

"We are now even," he said.

My mood brightened. "Oh, are you willing to admit I saved you on the train?"

Finn nodded. "You did me a service. I am glad to return the favor, but we should not make this a habit." He lowered his stare for emphasis.

"As if any of this is by design," I countered. "If Mother Nature wants to take down a cliff, who are we to stop her?"

Finn let that one sink in as we retraced our steps, heading down the path. "If anyone's a match for Mother Nature, it is you."

I decided it was a compliment but did not comment. Some things should be left to interpretation, or the truth could upset. Finn had saved the day. I was grateful, but I'd not come on this journey to turn into a simpering miss who batted her eyelashes at a man's remarkable strength or an almost kiss if that had even happened. If the situation had been reversed... hmm... I might have snatched him out of thin air. Or... we'd more likely have fallen like rag dolls down the cliff.

No matter. I'd marvel over Finn's quick thinking later. For now, the results of our little expedition had to be tallied. The count would not be positive. The map overlay had already been retrieved from its hiding spot—if it had ever existed. I'd have to believe it did, and Father or his partner had found the item. It would take several outings to determine if all four overlays had been retrieved.

"Drat!" I muttered.

"What's that?" Dori sang, having far too much energy while all turned to rot around us. "Did you also notice the men waiting for us at the buggy?"

I stopped on the narrow path, peeking between two spindly tree trunks. They offered a view downward where our buggy awaited. Finn had hired it. Quite an extravagant gesture, but it saved so much time. Standing beside the buggy were three men. We had not hired them, and their arrival was more than curious.

Several yards behind them was a wagon. Its two horses had been unhitched to let them cool down in the afternoon heat. The wagon was covered with a tarp, so I could not see within. Its back appeared open but offered no clue as to its purpose.

"They've been waiting for us," I gasped, turning to assess Finn's reaction. "Who are they?"

"Land Office Police." His lips spread into a thin line.

Having never heard of Land Office Police, I could only infer who they were by his tone... and it wasn't good.

FINN

"The Land Officers don't bite... much!"

My soft chuckle should have clued Willa in that she hadn't missed a vital piece of common knowledge. "Leave the officers to me. They are part of the Department of Interior, or the Department of Everything Else, as they are jokingly called. They're supposed to protect the nation's natural resources and cultural heritage."

None wore a uniform, and they looked more like thugs than lawmen. Of course, the guns strapped to their waists gave me pause.

"What national resources are in Kansas City?" Willa asked. "They look more like government treasure hunters."

"Don't say that to their faces," I said, but she had a point.

We made our way down the path, still taking care, but I shouted and waved for the men's attention. One of them acknowledged us with a hand held high. I decided he was in charge.

"Let me do the talking," I whispered as we neared the officers.

"Oooh," Dori sighed, "so many adorable men in one spot."

"I'm sure they're more charming from a distance," Willa said, pulling her roommate to her side and slowing their progress.

"I didn't say I wanted to take one home," Dori smirked, giving every indication that she did.

The Land Officers's stern expressions would clash with Dori's exuberance, so I walked ahead. It only took a short exchange to learn their purpose. It was worse than I'd thought. Turning to Willa, I sent her a look that said all I couldn't with words. I saw my silent news play across her features. A lump formed in my throat. We were developing a shorthand. Her expressive eyes read my glance, and I knew she knew—the police were there because of her father.

The officers motioned to the back of the wagon. The one in charge ushered Willa to stand beside him. Head high, she complied, and the air around us grew stale. Heat cloaked the scene, even disturbing the flies. Several hovered in one spot, practically stunned by the afternoon heat.

I moved next to Willa, whispering, "They've found another body and believe you can identify him."

A question stalled on her lips. They twitched, and I guessed she wanted to ask why, even though she had to know the answer. I still wanted to be the one to tell her... to break it as gently as possible.

"They found papers on him," I said, my voice dripping with regret. "You have been linked with Cornelius Abbot and are no longer protected by anonymity."

"But why have they brought a dead man to me?"

I sighed. "The police believe he is your father."

She briefly closed her eyes.

I dared to touch her arm. "You are the only one who knows him on sight."

Looking up at me, Willa tried to speak, but nothing came out. If only I could comfort her. Instead, dread seized my heart. I could do nothing to ease her pain.

"I'll be right here," I said, although I doubted my presence would help.

Every second sent a shock through my body as the Land Officer stepped back, allowing Willa the closest spot to the back of the wagon. A smell hit us first. I braced for it, knowing the scent would cling to our clothes long after. The body lay flat on his back, the head nearest the wagon's edge, feet facing the front. I noticed a mole on the side of the man's neck and the color of his hair, a tawny brown peppered with gray. The clothes were unremarkable. I'd expect better for a New Yorker.

Willa flinched at the sight of the body, which would be shocking in any circumstance, but identifying a family member? I regretted that she had to go through this. Remarkably, she studied the man's face.

Deep purples and blues were already forming on one cheek. I looked for a family resemblance but figured she took after her mother's side of the family. A flash of red caught the sunlight, drawing my attention to the corpse's left hand. It draped over a rounded chest. The pinkie finger wore a ruby ring. The gem stood for passion, prosperity, and protection. I guessed it only worked for the poor sot on two counts.

A sigh escaped Willa's lips as if the sun flooded her senses. She couldn't take her eyes off the dead man's ring. "I helped Mother pick out the trinket," she murmured, "for Father."

TWELVE

WILLA

"She's in shock!"

Dori held my hand during a rather rough buggy ride. She sat next to me. Worry marred her usual happy face. On my other side, Finn drove the one-horse rig. He glanced at me briefly, keeping any thoughts about my state of mind to himself.

"I'm so sorry," I mumbled.

"Sorry?" Dori squeezed my hand. "We are the ones filled with sorrow. I cannot imagine the jolt of seeing your father in such a state."

The dead body in the back of the wagon flashed in my mind's eye. The complete stillness of the poor soul, needing no air, left me speechless. It had worked in my favor, as I could only nod to the police. Just one little movement that caused a flurry of activity. They seemed quite pleased to have identified the body. "I am the one who is utterly sorry," I tried to explain, "as that man was not my father."

I looked down at the palm of my free hand. In it was my father's ring. Odd, as it was not the one he always wore. He favored a gold signet ring for practical reasons. He used it to seal sensitive correspondence, pressing his initials into hot wax. The ruby was sentimental. The Land Officer had given it to me. Perhaps I should feel bad about that kindness since I had fibbed about the dead man, although I had not lied about the ring. It belonged to Father, but that was where any connection ended.

Finn pulled on the reigns and stopped the buggy. He turned to me. "You lied to us?" Hurt stung his words.

Dori released my hand to cover her mouth. She almost muffled a gasp. Eyes wide, she didn't speak. Her look said it all.

I cringed. "The lie was for the Land Office Police," I explained. "I am telling you the truth now, as I could not tell you in front of the policemen without giving all away."

Their shock shifted to confusion. I sensed any strong emotions softening and hoped they would not be disappointed in me for too long. Finn, especially, had a stormy countenance.

"You lie quite easily," he said, not revealing if it was a compliment or a reproach. "Why did you do it?"

The story being rather long, I wished for a better moment to go into it all. We still had a journey to get back to the Harvey House. The short version would have to do, so I quickly told them about my father's favorite bedtime story. He delighted to share an adventure about how a man evaded his attackers by causing a diversion with lookalikes. Men that looked so alike, no one could tell the difference.

"That's a child's bedtime story?" Dori shrieked.

Finn hid a smile, clearing his throat. "The ring?"

I held it out to him. "It belongs to Father, and I knew he must have given it to this man, who looked very much like him, I might add." I gulped, feeling a rush of shame. "Father is in a terrible mess to employ a lookalike, but not for a minute do I believe he'd want anyone harmed in his stead."

Nodding, Finn seemed to understand, even if he still eyed me with some trepidation. "So, you said it was him to keep him safe. You are nothing if not loyal. Loyal to a fault."

His reprimand, wrapped in a compliment, left me cold. I'd damaged his trust.

"Willa is a good daughter," Dori said in my defense, showing her undeniable loyalty.

I could have hugged my roommate.

"I am worried your father is not worthy of such a daughter," Finn said. His hands fiddled with the reigns. "You have lied to the police, and it will come to light. Lies always do."

Contradicting him seemed inevitable, so I touched his forearm to lessen the blow. "I never said he was Father, so if they assumed I did, the fault is theirs. I only said the ring was Father's."

"You're not a simpering miss," Finn said, "nor capable of convincing the police that you were overcome in the moment and made a mistake. They will see through any act. Your lie has put us smack-dab in the middle of your father's mess."

I could think of no way to defend myself against his statement. Instead, I took in the scenery. We'd stopped along a stretch of dusty road that allowed a view of Kansas City's bluffs. Much of the rough terrain had been painstakingly graded or removed, which allowed the population to grow. However, the work would need to continue. I could see several areas where ravines cut into the limestone. Over time, they'd be as pronounced as the bluff we'd climbed. The erosion was an endless hand that shaped the area in the most harsh and majestic ways.

The vista held no interest for Finn. He neither cared for my excuse, pushing it aside as a minor technicality that no lawman would give credit. "When they determine your duplicity, you must answer for it."

Dori sniffed, "I'm sure a Pinkerton Man could smooth things over."

"Will you expose my lie?" I asked, worried about his answer.

"They will not hear it from me." He flicked the reigns, and the horse lurched into a trot, propelling us into a dangerously fast speed.

I rocked in the seat, falling toward Finn. He took pity on me, reaching a hand around my waist. The move practically locked me to his side. I dared a look at Dori, concerned that she'd see our improper closeness, but she was half turned away. Her death grip on the seat's armrest took all her attention.

"Oh my!" Dori cried at the pace of the buggy.

Finn finally came to his senses and slowed the horse's pace. Without a word, he released me. I inched away from his side. His temper might have gotten the best of him, but he'd done me a kindness. I peeked at him, trying to determine how long he'd stay mad. The day had been trying, yet it could not be helped. To not speak would have been wrong.

"I want to set a trap!"

Hands tightening on the reigns, Finn did not stop us a second time, but his teeth clenched in the most awful way. It practically gave me a toothache.

"Hear me out," I begged.

"Have I even heard right?" he scoffed, eyes on the road.

"What? What did you say?" Dori asked, uncertain of my declaration.

I'd been turned to Finn, and she could not have heard me clearly, not at the horse's pace. The air rushed over the buggy, over us. The only protection from the elements was a folding canopy, but it was down. The wind ripped at our hair, clothes, and any spoken word. I'd have to explain myself to each of them, but Finn's reaction mattered the most, as I felt sure Dori would follow me into Hell—with a smile—bless her!

I begged Dori to give me a moment, turning to Finn. "They must want the map."

"They?" Finn's single-word sentence was full of innuendo.

"Yes, they, as I do not know who seeks the map," I said, annoyed by his attitude. "A trap is the solution to bring them out of hiding. They must want the map. Father had to believe no one knew of the house, but now they must. They are on to him and possibly have all the overlays. They will be desperate to find the map and reunite all the pieces."

With a grunt, Finn discounted my assessment. "We have no evidence that anyone is against your father."

"If no one is against him," I reasoned, "then you are insinuating it is all my father's doing?"

"I'm saying it directly." Finn didn't mince words. "Your father could be behind it all."

I punched him in the arm. Finn stared down at me, shocked. I'd surprised him, which made the pain in my knuckles feel a bit better. Well, only a tiny bit. I'd never punched anyone before and would not do so again. I appeared to be the only one who suffered. The impact had little effect on Finn's solid muscle. Indeed, he was part cement!

Dori chuckled. She'd seen more than heard, but she understood body language. "Serves you right, Mister Finn."

"Indeed," I rallied, pressing my point. "Father would not kill his partner, nor would he kill a man he hired to imitate him."

"Why not?" Finn asked, blustering. "Outside of him being your father, we have no evidence of his good character. He could have wanted his partner out of the way, and he very easily could have hired a lookalike and killed him to fake his own death."

I cried out! Not because of Finn's assessment but because I'd suddenly realized the police might contact my mother. Mistakenly, of course, they would alert her that her husband had died. I had to send word before she got the horrifying news.

"You see my point now?" Finn asked, sounding regretful for taking me to task.

I would have punched him in the arm again had my knuckles not reminded me of that folly. "No, it's not what you said, but what I thought," I told him. "I must address a matter as soon as we return to the Harvey House." I took a quick breath, turning to Dori. "My mother."

Dori's eyes widened. "Oh my, yes, she must not hear of your father's demise. She will be told he expired and get a terrible shock."

"I have to send word," I said, keen to protect her from bad news, even if it exposed my own duplicity. It could not be avoided.

"You can't be so naive about your father," Finn interrupted.

Sitting in the middle of our threesome was getting out of hand. I could not address one without the other being greeted with my back. I swiveled around to squint at Finn. "Father would have more than one lookalike. They are to be a distraction, not a scapegoat."

Finn narrowed his gaze, as well. "Time will tell."

"Yes, and I shall expect an apology about my father's good name and intentions."

Finn growled to himself, focusing on the horse and our progress. He was like a dog with a bone he couldn't chew through. It was not a trait I admired, and he fell several notches in my regard.

The realization pained my heart as I wondered how far I'd fallen in his. If the buggy's speed was any indication, it was quite a bit as the pace picked up once again. Our outbound trip had taken a considerable stretch of time, but our return would be far less. The city streets were already in view.

I sat back, finding any more talk to be detrimental. After all, I knew what had to be done. Finn's good impression of me was already dashed, and whatever he thought, I'd not journeyed to Kansas City for the likes of a man. Well, not a handsome Pinkerton Man. I'd come to save my father, and no one would derail that goal!

We arrived at the Harvey House, kicking up a dust cloud. Finn jumped down, offering a hand to Dori and me. We alighted, turning to thank him again for the outing. Despite almost falling off the cliffside, seeing my first dead body, and doing irreparable damage to our relationship, it had been an incredible outing. I said as much, ready to retreat upstairs and plot my next step.

Finn blocked the way. "You will not set a trap," he ordered.

My hands approached my hips, and I'm sure a steely glare settled in my hazel eyes. I had been told several times that my determination was equal to that of a mama bear. A compliment, if I'd ever heard one.

"Now, now," Finn spoke first, "you have an uncanny knack for putting yourself in harm's way. If you continue down this path—of setting a trap—you will only do so if I am present."

"Oh," I said, letting my arms fall to my sides. Had I misjudged him? "That would be most welcomed."

How did that happen? Finn and I were suddenly in total agreement, and I wasn't yet ready to realize it had all been his doing. Such a state, however, took us both by surprise. We didn't know what to say to each other.

Luckily, Dori piped up. She raised a finger, daring to step between us. "May I make a suggestion?"

Standing on the sidewalk near the street entrance to the Harvey House, we were putting on a spectacle. Not that many were around to see, but we weren't the only Harvey Girls returning from a day off.

"The ride back gave me time to think," Dori said, not waiting for permission. "It is quite possible that the map is a complete ruse."

Thirteen

Willa

"The treasure map's fake?"

Finn's question hit hard, but that's what I'd heard Dori say, too.

"What do you mean?" I blustered, turning on my roommate and demanding the full story.

"The runes, it's all about the runes. The map and overlays are secondary," Dori said with a genuine smile as if it all made sense.

"You'll need to explain a little more," Finn coaxed.

Dori stepped closer to us, lowering her voice. "The map and the overlays probably don't lead to the treasure."

Seriously doubting we should be discussing such matters for any passerby to hear, I cleared my throat and invited Finn to join us inside. We quickly retreated to the drawing room, which luckily was empty. I could hear the din of the dining room crowd, so all were engaged in the everyday business of the Harvey House. We could talk in private.

"Please explain," I asked Dori, beginning to think of her as my treasure map expert.

Taking a seat in a winged-back chair, Dori left the loveseat for Finn and me. I noticed he sat on it like most men, taking up the majority of space. I perched on the edge, not wanting to give the impression that there was anything between us.

"Back on the cliff, before you almost plunged to your death, but Mister Finn saved you," Dori began, with me wanting her to skip that part, "we found the rune carved into the stone."

She was right. In all the commotion of getting off the bluff and being greeted by the police, I had forgotten about the symbol carved into the rock. "How does that change the purpose of the map?"

"The map was clearly meant to lead to four overlays," Dori explained, "but it really led to the rune. I expect each location to contain a rune, the real clues. The overlays, if they ever existed, are a misdirection. Thus, the map has already served its purpose. Your father had it pinned to a wall, you said. How important could it have been to him? He must have already known."

Finn and I thought on the matter. Dori sat and smiled at us, giving no indication she minded. I finally threw up my hands.

"Very well, the map was only the first part of the puzzle," I practically whined, "but we must work for the next ten days straight before we are allowed another day off. We can't wait that long to find the other runes."

A heaviness hung in the air between us.

"I will go," Finn offered. "I will visit the three other spots to search for more runes, but only if you promise to wait patiently, work at the Harvey House, and await my return. You must promise not to take any action to locate your father or his lookalikes or anything relating to the deaths or the treasure or anything. Am I clear? All must cease while I am away."

The air in the small drawing room felt charged with his request. Not for the first time, I wondered how Finn had weaseled his way so far into my life. I'd let him, of course, but he exceeded the scope of helpful into annoying. Yes, he saved my life. Drat him. It didn't mean he could treat me like an underling.

"You are hardly being reasonable," I said. "Time is important, and doing nothing is deadly."

Finn slowly placed his hands on his legs, giving them a tap. He was either impatient or restless. "If you insist, the runes must wait, and I will stay close to keep you out of trouble."

I jumped to my feet. "You will do no such thing!"

Finn moved just as fast, and we stood toe-to-toe, neither willing to back down.

"You overstep, sir!" I gritted out the words.

Finn's voice dropped low, threatening. "You won't be happy until you get yourself killed!"

Dori clapped her hands together. We looked at her, shaken out of our strong emotions. "I've never seen two people so in love," she beamed at us.

I can genuinely say Finn's shocked expression mirrored my own.

"You only want the best for each other," Dori said as if it were the sweetest thing.

I shrugged a shoulder, eyelids fluttering. Dori had a point, but I didn't want to be the first to say so.

Finn hung his head. "I will find the runes," he muttered.

"And I will not lure any killers out of hiding," I mumbled.

He nodded, seeming mollified, and I showed him to the door. Before he slipped out, Finn grasped my hand. "I'm trusting you," he whispered. "Don't break my heart by getting yourself killed."

Our eyes locked, but he slipped out before I could reassure him.

Dori came over and hugged me from the side. "I'm so glad you'll wait for Finn's return."

"I never said that," I exclaimed. "We have no time to waste! I am setting a trap!"

DORI

"You promised."

I reminded Willa for the hundredth time that she had indeed promised Finn not to set a trap for the killer.

"Of course, you are right," Willa said. "I promised Finn that I'd wait for his return; however, he is making three trips to find all the runes—which could take three days. It's an eternity."

Time was not on our side, so I had to agree, but setting a trap was a terrible idea. I had to talk some sense into my roommate. "A trap could backfire," I insisted.

"How can we wait?" Willa asked, dumbfounded by my argument. "Within three days, evil men could close in and attack my father. What if they kill him this time or another lookalike? Father might not be so lucky the next time, for he's certainly almost been captured twice."

Unable to dissuade Willa on that point, I pressed on the other. "But who is after your Father? We don't know."

Willa huffed, unable to answer. She had no idea who pulled the strings and wanted to find the Spanish treasure. No one knew all the players.

"What if we use this time to set up the trap?" Willa asked, warming to the idea. "We will only spring it once Finn returns."

I frowned at my roommate, too smart to be fooled. She knew we'd have little control once the plan came together. It could easily take on a life of its own. Maybe Finn would return in time to assist us, or he wouldn't. Only time would tell. Tricky, woeful time.

"We'd be blind, not knowing whom to trust." I pleaded with Willa to see reason. Her father's allies and foes were primarily unknown. Several could live in town and descend on us without warning. There was also a teeny tiny possibility that Willa's father might not be worthy of her trust.

Finn's accusation had to be considered, although I'd not plead the case with Willa. No daughter should be put through that unnecessarily. While finding Cornelius Abbot was the ultimate goal, I dared not think of the consequences if he betrayed his daughter's trust. Our ruse might attract him, as well as the other players, and we could be horribly surprised to find him behind everything.

No matter what, I'd protect my friend.

"We can draw them out with the treasure map." Willa rubbed her hands together as if she envisioned a successful plan. "The most straightforward way is to mention the map to everyone who comes through the Harvey House."

"A match to dynamite would be less volatile," I complained. "You have no way to control the spread of information. It most certainly could double back on us in the most hazardous way."

Willa tilted her head, giving me the distinct impression that she wasn't listening. She was planning. Oh dear, my clever roommate had an outrageously dangerous plan brewing, and she'd not be deterred. The situation seemed to be spiraling out of control. I feared that I could do little to alter the path, especially when I saw the determination in her pretty face. It sent shivers up and down my spine.

FOURTEEN

WILLA

"I'll lure out the killer and my father!"

When I explained my plan to Dori, I could see no flaws, only the added benefit of finding my father. He had to be in town. Once I unleashed news of the treasure map, he would hear and come out of hiding just in time to see the killer caught.

All politeness, Dori listened. She'd stop warning me of all the pitfalls, and for that, I was thankful. We'd heard nothing from Finn. It was for the best, as he might derail my plans and continue to blame my father for all the unseemly events. I could not believe as much. Of course, I had no proof but my heart, which sometimes was wrong.

To be honest, another emotion pulled at me, equally heartfelt. It pushed me to trust Finn more than I should. He'd come out of nowhere to champion my search, and I was grateful, yet a worry whispered in my ear. *Be wary*, it said.

More troubling. I'd sent a message to my mother, warning her that she might receive word of Father's demise. I assured her it was not true. I expected a return message any day, full of her shock and horror that I was in Kansas City and not visiting our friends in Philadelphia. It was a small fib I'd told her.

"You know I am right, no matter the spin you put on your actions," Dori pressed. "You promised Finn to be a good Harvey Girl and wait for his return."

"I am being good and working," I said, snapping out of my befuddlement and taking more care as I ironed my apron. It completed my Harvey Girl uniform. The bell would sound any moment. I only had enough time to put on the apron and tie my ponytail with a bit of matching starched white linen.

"You will not listen," Dori whined.

I tried to reassure my roommate. Alas, she already knew me too well. "Fear not, I am the only one breaking my word. Finn will not blame you."

"He cares for you," Dori said, clearly trying to make me feel bad for lying.

Melancholy gripped me, but a sizzling heat swiftly flooded over it. "Mister Finn Morgan is not my boss, kin, nor keeper. Thus, he holds no purchase on my endeavors, and if I must lie to stress that point, it is not truly a lie, but the act of protecting myself from a person that has encroached where they don't belong."

"He belongs," Dori muttered.

Taking pity on my friend, I complimented her faith in Finn. I liked him, as well, and said as much.

Dori gaped at me. "If you go through with your plan, Finn will never be your husband!"

Of all the arguments she could have made, that one danced over my last nerve. "Husband?" I gasped, feeling a flush on my cheeks.

Dori huffed, quite upset with me. "You could do worse."

The bell sounded, and not another word could pass our lips, even though I had a few to share. Instead, we rushed downstairs to our positions in the Harvey House dining room. Twelve of us hurried to our spots, looking like the proper, respectable ladies Fred Harvey had envisioned when he set up his business. We added a refinement to the dining experience, and even though my mind raced with thoughts of trapping the despicable men responsible for two murders, I put on my biggest, brightest smile to greet our guests.

I'd moved from assisting Shirley to serving the diners directly with my own mentee. The young girl's wide eyes waited for my hand signals, eager to please. I thought her name was Rose, but I'd been told when my thoughts were elsewhere. It really didn't matter. We never used our names.

"Willa Abbot!" A male voice said my name as if spotting a long-lost friend.

I spun around, still smiling, as it was the first greeting any Harvey Girl gave a customer, even one with a booming voice. The dining room was crowded with train passengers. They had barely twenty minutes at our stop and wanted to leave with a full belly to serve them for the rest of their trip.

My eyes flew wide as I recognized the young man. "Kip Hollingshead?"

The cocky little gossip sat down at an open seat. Unfortunately, it was right in front of my station at the bar. I would have no way to avoid a conversation with a man who traveled in my social circles. Running across someone I knew, even as indirectly as Kip, was always possible. Unfortunately, whatever I said would become fodder for his next party in New York City. We were not close enough for him to keep my secret. Quite the opposite. He knew me just enough to relish my situation and dine out gossiping about me for months!

"Fancy meeting you here," Kip chuckled. "It took me a moment to register your lovely face, as it is so out of place in this establishment. I must say, is life so boring that you have come to this?"

The matron's eyes were on us. I could feel them, not needing to turn. They bore into my skin, always concerned with the service, its excellence, and its speed. Anything but brief exchanges were frowned upon. The train waited for no man, and if I threw off a passenger with talk—even if they instigated it—the blame would be mine.

"Shall you have a steak today?" I asked Kip. "It is marvelous and will serve you well for the rest of your journey."

He nodded, agreeing to the feast. "With all the fixings," he added. "And coffee, black."

I signaled Rose, and she quickly handed me the correct plates. From my point of view, I placed a coffee cup at the four o'clock position. Its spot was also part of the code, signaling my assistant which beverage to pour. Five o'clock was tea. Six o'clock was milk. Seven o'clock was prune juice. I had no idea how to signal for help, not that anyone could aid me with this particular dilemma.

Kip attacked his food, munching with some exaggeration. "Won't say, will ya? As you wish. I assume it is a dark family secret. The Abbots always aim too high for the nut."

My smile might have agreed, but my eyes did not.

Digging a fork into the crispy hash browns, Kip scrunched his nose at me. "The apple does not fall far from the tree."

No fan of Ralph Waldo Emerson's saying, I only nodded as I served other passengers. He raised his empty coffee cup, and I returned to him. Something about the look in his eye made me pause and not signal Rose for the refill.

"Skip it." He set the cup back down, lowering his voice. "I am half a mind not to let you in on a secret, you being a lady and all. It's not proper, but it is you, after all. And it's about your father. He's in the worst kind of trouble."

Something about his gossip rang true. "Tell me," I begged.

"He is wanted for murder." Kip smiled. His glee was unsettling.

I shook my head. It could not be, for if Kip had heard such news, Finn must have also. Had he kept the whole truth from me? Or was this a new development? I calculated when the gossips would have gotten the information, giving it enough time to become part of the idle talk that Kip would hear, and realized Finn would have been in town during that time—not yet away looking for the runes. After returning from our outing, he'd taken a day to prep for his search and allow Dori to study the map for the other rune locations. Once armed, he'd set off, and we'd not heard from him since—nor had we expected to. It had been two days.

It dug at my heart, considering Finn's loyalties. Would they be to me or the law? Of course, Kip's gossip might not be valid. I held onto the fact and faith that Finn would not hide such vital information. We had bonded... even though I had not known him long—and we were a bit on the outs. I could trust Finn. I counted on the fact. On the other hand, Kip was a toad who should not be trusted.

Kip gave me a pointed look, one tempered with fake understanding. "Imagine my surprise, having such bad tidings whispered by another passenger on my trip home. I could not believe it at first, but they said it had to do with a treasure. I believe your father has again fallen to the lust for lost riches."

Shame overwhelmed me. I wondered how long it would take to reach Mother. "Oh my, Kip," I said. "Are you allowing yourself to be swept up in gossip again? I believe you have fallen to such errors before. I would not want you to look the fool again, as I have been in the company of a Pinkerton Man and am privy to local police concerns."

Kip sat back on his stool, surprised.

"I assure you," I said, my chin titled upward, a firmness in my jaw, "my Father is not wanted for any crime."

Kip snorted. "You being here says otherwise, unless there is another reason to be a Harvey Girl? A bet lost or some such? Come, explain. Why are you here? No, don't tell me; it will just be a lie. You have that in common with your Pinkerton Man. They lie a lot."

The possibility struck me. *Not Finn*, I thought.

"That is exactly what Pinkerton Men do to get the goods. They lie, and why wouldn't such a man lie to you if he was tracking your father?" Kip nodded at me like he knew the ways of the world. "You have probably led the police—and this Pinkerton—right to your father. Oh my, Willa, you have stepped in it now."

I gasped as truth rang in his words. I had to second guess why Finn had spent so much time helping me to find the treasure. After all, I'd claimed over and over again that it would lead to Father. With a sinking feeling, I knew I'd been fooled.

FIFTEEN

WILLA

"Finn is a traitor!"

I threw out the accusation, not willing to hear it contradicted. Not that many people had the opportunity. Only two of us were in the room. Our room upstairs at the Harvey House.

Dori sighed. "How can you believe such a thing? It originated from a man you called a toad."

It was not the first time that Dori had argued on Finn's behalf. I refused to listen. Bullheaded, perhaps, but after two days of talking up the treasure map, I felt ready to spring my trap. Time was running out. An inner clock ticked away at the time my plans could help or hinder

Father. I had to act, especially if Finn had been working against me all along.

I kept flip-flopping back and forth on that dilemma, but Finn would be back soon. If there was even a slight chance that he'd ruin my plans and stand against Father, I needed to act before his return.

"Finn is in love with you," Dori insisted. "The last thing he'd do is put your father in danger, even if he believed the worst of him. And I must point out that we might need his muscles."

She had a point—not about Finn's affections. He added a level of strength that was impressive. All we had were our wits. I quickly reminded myself that battles were won with strategy more than might, although one could not discount a canon ball.

A hard rapping sounded on our door. I shared a look with my roommate, and she quickly slipped under her covers. Ready for bed, she left it to me to answer the insistent knocks. I didn't blame her. The harsh sound signaled trouble, but I opened the door anyway.

Mrs. Agnes Q. Downs filled the doorframe. Her unwelcoming frown marked a setback. I felt we'd progressed, and she admired all my hard work at the Harvey House. None of that shone in her steely glare.

"Talk of Spanish gold has been riling up guests and girls," she said, pinning me with another withering look. "It seems to be originating from you." She insinuated catastrophe with her tone of disgust.

A fib might be expected in such a situation, as it had worked for me on other occasions. However, I recognized the tone. Mrs. Downs wasn't asking. She knew. I had hardly been discreet, as time was not on my side.

"Is it really all that bad?" I asked with an innocent smile. "I have been seeking advice and a bit of local history."

Mrs. Downs scoffed, looking at Dori, whose shock appeared genuine. She sat up in bed, a patchwork quilt pulled around her for comfort more than warmth. Showing uncanny instincts, my roommate maintained a neutral expression. I doubted she'd speak unless directly questioned.

"Is that wrong?" I feigned confusion, hoping I could pull it off. The innocent act rarely worked on women. "I was only trying to find out more of the town's history to aid in the search for my father. He, unfortunately, seems to be caught up in the Spanish treasure."

"Pitty-pat, missy." Mrs. Downs flapped a hand at me. "You will resist any more talk on the subject. It is unbecoming of a Harvey Girl."

Having evoked the ultimate evil for anyone working at the Harvey House, I had little recourse. My head bowed. I tried to look contrite, wheels turning on how to outmaneuver the accusation. Nothing viable came to mind. Drat!

"You are stirring up a hornet's nest," Mrs. Downs said. She wagged a finger at me.

I used the gesture to stare at her shoes. They came to a dramatic point, making me worry for her toes. It was rather hard to think in the face of the matron's feet and rage.

"You've disrupted the whole town," she continued. "I fear it will erupt in a fury of speculators, as it once did. A very shameful, trying time for Kansas City. We look down on fortune hunters. No good will come of it!"

I made an uh-oh face, as I did not wish to spark more treasure hunters. I just wanted to lure out the one related to me. I knew it to be a consequence, but Mrs. Downs did not need to know that I knew.

"Beg my pardon, ma'am," I said.

Her ample chest puffed out. "If I hear another word, you will be out. Do you understand?"

I nodded, and seeing how the Harvey House was central to my plans, I would heed her warning. Besides, I'd already spread the treasure map's existence to enough people. If my father or the unsavory sorts connected to the treasure map were nearby, they'd hear and act.

"I expected more from you," Mrs. Downs finished. "And I hope that lumpy mess is not how your bed usually appears." She squinted at the lumps under my bedcover. Without another word, she turned on one heel and stomped down the hallway.

Several doors carefully closed, reopening in her wake. Wisely, no one wanted to face her in such a mood. I peeked out, catching a few annoyed faces. No one appreciated my efforts to stir up trouble. I smiled at the girls and shut my door as if nothing was wrong.

"Well, if that doesn't convince you," Dori stammered, "nothing will."

It seemed rude to contradict her. I went to my lumpy bed and flung back the quilt. Under it, bedsheets were tied together, one end knotted to the bed frame's metal foot. I tugged at it, dragging the whole bed to the window.

Dori sighed. "You're still going?"

I opened the window and threw my makeshift bedsheet rope out the opening. I had only planned to test the rig but couldn't wait another second. "I can't quit now." The very idea was inconceivable.

"Yes, you could," Dori wailed.

I found her caution disheartening since she'd had my back so many other times. "I must go tonight. I doubt I'll get another chance. Besides, Father could be waiting at the house."

"Trouble could be waiting," Dori corrected me.

"Perhaps both," I said, "since I did my best to let everyone know I had a Spanish treasure map and would be at the house."

I never said it was a safe plan.

Rushing over to Dori's bed, I gave her a quick hug. "Never fear," I told her.

"What should I do if you don't return before morning?" Dori blinked at me.

She seemed to be conjuring the worst results. Possibly ones that had me beheaded or trapped by a hoard of treasure hunters. Neither appealed to me, so I forced such negative thoughts out of my mind.

"I promise not to do anything silly," I assured her.

Dori choked: "You are already the most reckless girl I know!"

While that might be the case, I saluted her and shimmied out the window. The wind swirled my skirt, but my carefully knotted sheets held firm. Within seconds, I landed on both feet, just another bit of darkness, ready to sneak away in the night. Looking up, Dori gave me a little wave and pulled the sheets back up and out of sight. I really owed her some consideration, as she was the most loyal of roommates.

"Psst!" Dori whistled.

I looked up again, and she tossed down the rolled-up treasure map. I'd almost forgotten it!

My smile was quite genuine as I hurried toward my father's house. The distance did not bother me, but the moon remained hidden, heavy clouds working against my vision. Only the street lamps and light from nearby homes helped to show the way. They were all pitiful, though. The darkness of the hour cloaked the neighborhood. The only positive—it hid my approach.

Taking care not to stumble, I jogged, breathing deeply, but eventually slowed to a walk. The mansion loomed ahead. Dark. Judgmental.

I wondered how to approach it without being seen. Despite the night sky, no direction would completely hide me, not if someone waited within. It could not be helped. Pushing care aside, I walked up the front stone path. However, before I reached the front steps, voices drifted to me. Bickering male voices.

Hunching down, I snuck closer. One of the voices sounded peeved. It rang a bit louder, gruffly repeating one point over and over: "The map," he said. "The map."

The other voice was lower. Calm. Calculating. "She will come, and the map will be ours."

A shiver ran down my spine. The man was correct. I'd come with the map. But that's not why I felt like a fool. The male voice rang with a British accent. It struck me that I'd lured notorious con men to my father's house. The ones I'd learned about on the train ride to Kansas City. Men that everyone, especially Finn, had warned me to avoid.

Not that I knew for sure, but I didn't want to find out by rushing into the house and right into their arms. Slinking backward, I made as little noise as possible.

The mansion's front door swung wide. A bear of a man filled the opening. And here I thought Mrs. Agnes Q. Downs was intimidating in such a stance, but the con man won the prize.

"Do come in," the bear growled.

The British one pushed past his companion. "We have much to discuss, lovey." His accent dripped with innuendo.

Oh my, Dori's worst fears would become reality—unless I acted fast!

Sixteen

Willa

"Your accent is charming."

I remained rooted on the front pathway, ten yards away from the Big Guy and the Brit. The con men scowled at me, standing in father's front door like they owned the place. Their names, mentioned in passing while traveling to Kansas City, evaded me. I'd heard them only once, and I desperately tried to pull out the information to use against them. Drat, my memory! And the flush of panic clouding my mind!

"Compliments won't get you far, love," the British ruffian said, pointing, "but if that's a treasure map in your hand, I'll be the charmed one."

His wink turned my stomach. For a Confidence Man, his skills were lacking. One usually heard of beguiling men who were able to tell a thumper. The tales made their targets willing to give away their money for nothing.

"Map, now," the big one said. His sheer bulk quivered with power, threatening to burst out of a tweed jacket.

"Not so fast," I said.

The Brit's upper lip quivered. "You're right daft, aren't you, love?" He winked again, more flirty than mad, but the tremor in his voice belied the nonchalance.

I didn't have long with this pair. They'd undoubtedly manhandle me, take the map and disappear. I couldn't let that happen without knowing what they knew of Father's whereabouts. Could they have been partnered in the treasure hunt? I had to know. However, I had to admit that they couldn't be in Father's pocket if they wanted the map. They didn't realize it was a Spanish mislead—a layer of protection.

Waving the map, I lifted my chin and chuckled. "This old thing? Come, come, are we not friends?" With a confident stride, I walked up the front steps toward them. I did belong there and acted like it. "Are we not cloth cut from the same bolt?"

I pushed past them, entering my father's house. They pivoted, startled, and allowed me to pass, following. The firm thud of the front door closing gave me pause, but I

continued into my father's office. It seemed the best spot
to spring the rest of my hasty plan.

Setting the rolled-up map on the desk, I took a
moment to light a lamp. While the home had electricity,
I favored oil. It cast long shadows about the room. Less
light meant a lesser chance of them seeing right through
me. I needed all the help I could muster to sell my pack
of lies.

Leaning against the desk, I turned to them. They
awkwardly stood before me, eyes flicking to the map.
Clearly, they didn't know if they should sit or take the
map and run. I had to convince them to hear me out.

"Shall we drop all pretense?" I asked, not giving them
a chance to answer. "The map is yet another Spanish tale.
Please tell me you have not fallen for it?"

The men shared a confused look.

"Come, come," I admonished them, "are you not in
my father's inner circle? When was the last time you
spoke with him?"

"Your father?" The Brit tugged at his ear. A tell for
sure, but precisely what it signaled, I could not guess.

"Who dat?" the big Brute asked.

My stomach dropped. "Egad! This is his house."

The Brit shrugged. "Nice, but we came for the map,
not a lesson about your family tree."

"Map!"

Their insistence on the treasure map confounded me. "I expected more from such a team," I hissed, their names popping into my mind with blinding relief, "as the great Sullivan & Tuck!"

The compliment hit its mark.

"You have heard of us?" the Brit said, pleased. His chest puffed out.

"Tuck & Sullivan," the Brute corrected, instantly clueing me who was who.

I nodded, guiding them back to what I needed to know. "You have met my father, correct?" I grabbed a family photo from his desk, pointing at his image. "Cornelius Abbot?"

They peered closer. Tuck's large head cocked to one side. Sullivan, in his clipped accent, said, "Never seen him. This is his house?"

"But we were sent here for the map," Tuck grumbled.

Frustrating on so many levels, I dared not let them digress. They'd said nothing. They knew nothing of Father! My heart sang. He was not working with them. My heart sunk. They would not know his location, presenting another dead end. "Who sent you after the map?"

"That ain't none of your business, is it?" Sullivan frowned.

Crossing my arms over my stomach, I had no intention of letting them leave without a fight. Well, one with words. I'd clearly lose any actual scuffle, although I had my eye on the fire poker. If the mood changed, I hoped to wield it like a sword, but I would probably only break a vase, knock over the oil lamp, and set the room on fire. That sounded more like me.

"The map is rot," Sullivan told Tuck. "We need to see the man about this. He led us wrong; he did."

Tuck snarled. It sounded like no good would come when they met with The Man.

"We must join forces," I implored. "I fear you will be duped, yet again, if you ignore my aid. For you see, I have a Pinkerton Man in my pocket and have quite led him, along with the Land Police, on a merry chase. But they are poking about, and Kansas City is not a safe place for the likes of us, if you know what I mean."

They did not, as their blank stares spoke volumes. Unsure if they weren't buying or weren't willing to take me into their confidence, I pressed on, giving them little chance to think it through. If I gave them too much time, even their limited number of brain cells would work it out.

"Just tell me one thing," I raised my voice, "who is The Man?"

Sullivan's lips curled in the most unattractive way. I wasn't sure if it was due to revealing the name to me or for the new distaste of the one pulling their strings. "He calls himself Reggie Brown. Knew we couldn't trust an East Ender."

Reggie Brown? My father's self-proclaimed business partner had been found dead—in this very house—but as I was fast learning, lies were more prevalent than flies when it came to treasure hunters.

SEVENTEEN

WILLA

"I'm a Confidence Man!"

I smiled, thinking it couldn't have happened to a more competent woman.

Dori gawked at my greeting. I'd barely given her time to enter our room, having just finished a long shift. She was dressed in a starched-to-perfection Harvey Girl uniform. No small fete after a full day serving diners.

Fearing I'd shocked her, I tried to make light of my statement. After all, it was our first chance to talk in detail. Last night, I could only give her the highlights. We needed some sleep to be fresh for work. I wanted to explain everything that had happened when I met with con men Sullivan & Tuck. "I know it sounds like I've fallen in with the worst kind of scoundrels, but they've accepted me. With their help, I'm sure to find my father."

Unfortunately, my roommate disagreed. "You're a con man? That's almost humorous, as I'm losing all confidence in you," Dori whined.

Her enthusiasm had sustained me so much that I didn't know what to say when faced with disapproval. It echoed in my ribcage like a trapped, hissing snake.

"Finn has returned," Dori added, plowing right through my distress with another blow. She'd hung back after our shift, and now I knew why. "He's downstairs."

The unexpected announcement made my heart and stomach ache for entirely different reasons. Of course, the Pinkerton Man was expected back, but in his absence, I did not heed his wishes and continued to search for my father. Not that I had to justify myself, but Finn might feel differently.

"Will you come down, too?" I begged for Dori's help. Men were a bit of a mystery to me, and she could be a buffer against uncomfortable questions.

"You need to do this alone," Dori said. "He likes you. Don't ruin it."

For once, her good-natured meddling hit a nerve. "You put too much faith in Finn Morgan."

"You put too much faith in your father," Dori said with a sigh. Her eyes, however, never wavered from mine. "Forgive me, but your father's actions—whether they are honorable or heartbreaking—are leading you down a dark path."

A prickly sensation sizzled across my skin as if I'd been burned. It faded quickly. Emotions were like that, making themselves known one minute and hiding away the next. No matter my shock, I had to respect Dori's opinion. She'd jumped right into my madness. I owed her.

"As you wish," I replied, regretting my joke about the con men. It had fallen flat.

As I headed downstairs to face Finn, I tried thinking of something clever—some way to control our first exchange. I needed to smooth over our last disagreement and possibly a new one. A simple plan evolved: I'd just let him talk about the Spanish treasure. The sun was setting; it was near curfew. Mrs. Downs would probably come and run him off. I'd leave his reproach for another day, giving myself another night to journey to Father's house and solve the mystery. Confident of my plan, I entered the small sitting room on the ground floor.

Finn waited inside. Alone. Slightly turned away from the door, he seemed to be studying the settee, perhaps lost in thoughts of how to handle me. I noticed the set of his jaw. Tight. Tense. I steeled myself; this could be trickier than I'd anticipated.

"Welcome back from your adventure," I forced a smile. Being phony wasn't in my nature, but desperate times. "You were away longer than expected."

"Disappointed?" Finn did not return my warm greeting. "Alas, you did not disappoint me."

Scrunching up my nose, my simple plan flew out the open window, which faced the street. We were as far as you could get from the train tracks, which wasn't far at any Harvey House. "You must have had a trying search. You've lost all your good manners."

"Forgive me." He clipped off each word. "I've been overwhelmed by tales of your adventures. Tell me more about the new friends you've made in my absence."

The intensity of his emotions radiated all around us—dizzying. I'd be stupid to get too close to him. Okay, I was foolish. I stepped toward Finn. He did, as well, squaring off for a battle.

"Friends is the wrong word," I waffled, momentarily confused how to proceed.

"The Land Officer we met saw you with two known Confidence Men." His head cocked to one side as if he couldn't bring my face into focus. He was standing rather close.

The small size of the room added to the intoxication, amplifying the scent of him. Freshly shaven. He'd cleaned up before coming to see me. Of course, he wouldn't have barged into the Harvey House restaurant during our busy hours. Making a scene wasn't his style, so he had time to look presentable. It didn't have anything to do with me.

"How clever to utilize the local police for stealthy observations," I said, hoping he understood sarcasm. By the instant frown on his full lips, he did. "Rather curious, indeed, to use them to watch me. What a waste."

"I was worried." Finn blinked, head tilting to the other side.

"Are you only here to express concern, or did you discover more about the Spanish treasure?" I asked, trying not to notice the intensity of his stare. It practically picked me off my feet.

His breathing quickened. "Don't you want my help?"

"I want you." The proximity of his body confused my mouth. Talking and even walking seemed impossible for a moment until I realized the implication of my words. "Your help, I mean. I want your help, of course, but I want my help, too."

Only inches separated us. It would have been so easy to place a hand on his broad chest, but I caught myself, not knowing if I wanted to shove him away or tug his shirt to draw him closer. Both urges were hard to repress. I didn't dare touch him when I had no idea which impulse would win. Instead, I stepped back, but he grasped my arms and pulled me within a breath of a kiss.

"Willa."

My name sounded like an omission of defeat. His tone called to a part of me I hadn't known existed. My hands moved to his chest, but something glittered in my peripheral vision. Just a tiny movement that played against the windowpane. A man stood outside the Harvey House, watching us from the sidewalk. A man I recognized—my father. And not one of the lookalikes. My real father.

FINN

Willa?

My voice cracked, and for one sweet moment, our eyes locked. She seemed to understand that I only wanted to help. However, something caught her eye. She looked out the window and gasped.

"Wait here," she begged and rushed to the door.

Every instinct told me to follow her, but I knew that would be folly. Forcing my help would not work with Willa. I had to let her come to me. Already, I feared I had pushed too hard. Tracking down the runes was necessary, but it took part of the mystery out of her hands.

We'd parted at odds, but I'd hoped three days would cool her temper and allow her to see things from my perspective. I had not attacked her father's good name; I only meant that his involvement could not be overlooked completely. Perhaps I could have taken more care. She was fiercely loyal, a quality I admired.

Whatever the outcome of her mood, I'd paid for leaving her alone so long. At the first opportunity, she'd sidestepped our meeting and run away. I peeked out the window, desperate to spy on the cause of her abrupt departure and not get caught in the act.

A man waited on the street outside. One that resembled Cornelius Abbot. Whether he was the real McCoy or a lookalike, I could not ascertain. I'd need Willa for that determination. If he was her father...

I couldn't finish the thought. As far as I knew, he'd committed no crime. To barge out onto the street and force the introduction could turn out badly. My wish... for Willa to bring the man inside and introduce us. If she cared for me...

I also could not finish that thought.

The door to the small parlor opened. Dori rushed in, followed by a stern-faced woman.

"Oh, Mister Morgan," Dori said, her voice higher than I remembered, possibly due to the older woman's presence.

"May I have the pleasure of presenting Mrs. Agnes Q. Downs, the Harvey House matron."

The woman in question squinted at me.

"Mister Finn Morgan, ma'am," Dori said with a courtesy.

It was one of the most elegant introductions of my life.

"A Pinkerton Man?" Mrs. Downs questioned.

I doubted she ever used more words than necessary. "Yes, Mrs. Down, but I am not here on Pinkerton business."

"What business are you here for?" Mrs. Downs drilled me with her stare. She could have interrogated a notorious convict and gotten a confession.

I quickly explained that I'd met Willa on the train and owed her a debt, as she had assisted me with a pickpocket. "I am helping her find her father." My smile beamed as I stepped to block the view out the window. The last thing Willa needed was to be spotted outside with a man. If he turned out to be her father, that was one thing. If not, disaster.

Dori scrunched up her nose. One eyebrow rose, and I distinctly felt she was onto my wish to protect Willa. She might not know why or how, but she came to my aid.

"Willa will be down shortly," Dori lied.

It had to be for the matron's benefit.

"I'll wait, if I may," I said.

Mrs. Downs nodded her head. "As long as there is no trouble."

I had no idea if Willa was in trouble, and I dared not look out the window.

"Oh, no," Dori smiled, "no trouble unless we lose dear Willa to the courting of an attractive Pinkerton Man."

I gulped.

"Take care," Mrs. Downs said, shaking a finger at me. "Our girls sign contracts, and Willa still has a long stint ahead. Don't go believing you can swoop in and win her hand. She deserves much better than that, do you hear me?"

I nodded, heart thumping, sweat breaking out across my brow.

Dori winked at me. She'd effectively protected Willa's machinations and given me a purpose for showing up at the Harvey House—as Willa's suitor! Whatever was happening outside couldn't be as bad as in the little parlor. I wished the fireplace would spit out flames and consume me whole.

EIGHTEEN

WILLA

"Father!"

I shouted, racing out onto the street.

Not knowing if Finn understood or followed my hasty departure, I darted outside the Harvey House, attempting to intercept my father. Looking up and down the street, I spotted his figure running away. Running away for me?

He headed toward his house, but I could not fathom the flight. Even wearing a long skirt, I could easily catch up to him. And I did, within a block of his home.

"Father," I shouted, "please, stop!"

He slowed until gravity pulled at his bones, causing a full stop. Working rather hard to catch his breath, Cornelius Abbot turned my way. His look was one of shock and dismay. I truly felt he had not known it was me until that moment.

"Willa, could it really be my only daughter?" He blinked, rubbing at his eyes.

"You can trust what you see," I assured him. "It is your daughter who has falsely identified a dead man as you. A lookalike of your own choosing, I have no doubt, although the police are uninformed on the matter."

A cloud settled on his continuance. He grumbled a bit before actual words formed. "Why did you identify the wrong man?"

"To protect my father."

"You put yourself in danger," he moaned.

I decided it was not my place to tell him the danger lay elsewhere, but he needed to know that I knew how to avoid trouble. "Lying to the police can be explained," I said, stating a simple but effective plan. "If they should discover the truth, I will own that I made a mistake, most certainly due to shock. After all, it was the first dead body of my acquaintance."

Father shook his head. I could not ignore how our time apart had aged him. The sag in his jaw held no joy, which was his usual appearance. "The danger is not from the Land Officers, my dear."

I believed the danger came from his assorted, despicable partners. "What are you doing in this conundrum?" I asked.

"The treasure is false, and you've certainly been duped or worse."

"What could be worse?"

"Are you part of the scheme?" I pulled no punches. While I would not allow others to besmirch my father, I had to know the truth. "Has circumstance contrived and made you part of this dastardly business? I must admit, you reek of it."

Father coughed, and I feared he needed a chair and strong spirits. The blow I'd delivered hit harder than I imagined. It signaled more distress for our family.

"Have I fallen so far that you would think so ill of me?" His eyes lowered to his shoes.

"You promised Mother, and you cannot tell me you kept it. Whatever this is, it is of your own making." I hated proving my point, but he could not wiggle out of his actions, even if my love for him would forgive anything.

"I will not contradict you, Willa, but I will implore you to go home." His voice turned stern, a sound I had never heard from him before. He was usually a most indulgent parent.

"I shall go nowhere until you tell me everything." Taking a step forward, I held my hand out and crooked the pinkie. It had been a handshake of ours from a very young age.

He did not notice the comforting gesture. Shame overtook his expression. He admitted in the lowest of voices, "They have used my name to fool the good people of this town. From the Mayor on down, they used the lookalike, bought a house, and killed the man they created, so I cannot even speak for myself. They created a man who is more me than me.

"Certainly, it can all be set right." I frowned. "You are you and must be able to prove it."

"Not in this city," Father wailed. "They took my signet ring, and it convinced the bank. They have set me up as an interloper not to be trusted. It is hopeless. Now, will you go home?"

"No."

Father coughed again, doubly shocked. I imagined he'd not heard that tone from me, either.

"No, you say?"

"I am not the Willa you left in New York. I am the woman who has come here to save you, even if it must be from yourself." I crossed my arms over my chest, every inch defiant.

I had no notion how my dear father would respond, and I may never know. A shot rang out!

We ducked, and someone shouted my name.

The thud of feet and the rush of at least seven men caused a commotion that knocked me to the ground. Eyes fluttering, I saw two thugs roughly pull my father away. A scream must have escaped my lips, for my throat painfully constricted. Arms grabbed me from behind, and everything went dark.

Nineteen

Willa

"You'll be leaving one way or another!"

The man's chilling threat tickled my memory. I'd heard that voice before. Of course, cockney accents were common in New York City, but we were still in Kansas City.

It didn't help that I had a bag over my head and wrists tied together. I'd never been so manhandled. Even worse, I missed some of the action. My head hurt from a bump, and the tops of my feet from being dragged more than carried to our new location.

Wherever we were, the air smelled dusty. It needed an airing out. Curled up on a hard floor, though, I had few clues to name the spot. I listened for more voices. Several men were present, but the threatening one was doing all the talking. Whatever had become of my father, I could not say. I hoped he had not been treated as rudely. Doubtful, as we'd most certainly been taken for nefarious reasons.

"You be understanding me?" the threatening man asked.

Whether the question was directed at me or another, I could not know for sure, but it had to end. My fate was my own to guide. I'd not leave it in the hands of these ninnies.

Sitting up on the floor, I moaned as my weight found a bruise. "Show yourself," I demanded. "For your threats are empty if nothing is known of the might that backs them."

The sack yanked up and away from my head, revealing the study in my father's Kansas City house. As I'd recently learned, the house had been purchased in his name and was not his doing. It looked as before, the empty spot on the wall practically shouting at me. It's where the Spanish treasure map had been pinned.

Candlelight greeted me with a soft glow, casting shadows that hid much of the room and its occupants. One man stepped forward—Reggie Brown. I'd met him on the train. He'd claimed to be my father's business partner and had initially directed me to this home. I could only believe I was part of his plan to use my father's name.

"Looking good for a dead man," I said, giving Reggie my most complimentary smile.

His belly shook with laughter, but my response threw him off. I could see it in the turn of his lip. "Don't be too clever, dear, or you'll miss all the fun."

"More threats," I said, unmoved. "You might have me and the real Cornelius Abbot, but you don't have the treasure map or the gold."

Beefy arms crossed his chest. "There is no gold."

"I know you believe there is no gold," I countered, "or is that just part of the act to fool your flunkies and keep it all for yourself?"

I counted five other men in the room and gave them a nod. More must be outside. They appeared rough, ready for a fight, and probably clueless about the treasure and Reggie's intentions. They certainly weren't expecting me or the suggestion that they were as dumb as geese flying North instead of South for the winter.

"You found the Spanish gold?" one of the ruffians complained. The others puffed out chests and waved a fist or two to show what they thought of being double-crossed.

"Don't listen to the chit," Reggie barked at them. "She knows nothing. We got a good thing going here and all we got to do is be smart."

I laughed at that as if he'd given me a gift to knock him down. "Oh, hey, you gonna let him call you dumb to your faces?"

"Who you calling dumb?" one brute grumbled.

"Yeah, Reg, we don't take to that kinda talk." Another backed up the first. He had a broken nose. At least, a strong jolt had twisted it at an awkward angle. Sadly, it had never been fixed.

"Boys, boys," Reggie tried to calm his men.

I interrupted, "You know Reggie's like a ghost. The police think he's dead, so if your scheme goes bad, who do you think will be blamed and tracked down like mad dogs?"

Eyes blinked, and for a minute, I wasn't sure they understood.

"You!" I quickly added, and the air in the room shifted. The men were on my side, and Reggie knew it.

"Who's gonna untie me?" I asked, raising my wrists to show off the ropes. "I have the real treasure map and can take you to the gold."

The mood shifted again as the lure of treasure piqued their desire. I bit my tongue, worried I'd gone too far.

Reggie raised his hands, trying to get their attention. "She don't know nothin' and that Spanish gold ain't never been found. It never existed." His nostrils flared. It was not an attractive look, but he was making some sense to the men.

I got to my knees. "You could not be more wrong, sir."

"The map is a fake!" Reggie nodded his head up and down at his men. "I had it made in San Francisco!"

With a slight tilt of my head, I sighed, almost taking pity on the scoundrel. "Well, then your mapmakers were clairvoyant because I followed the map to the bluffs and found an old Spanish rune etched into the mountainside. It was a second clue to an overlay that, once combined with the map, led me to the treasure." Honestly, I was starting to believe my lie. So were the men.

Reggie pointed an accusing finger at me. "All that gold and you're still here? I think not!"

I turned pouty lips to the men. "You duped and endangered my most beloved father, sir; some things are more dear to a tender heart than gold."

The nearest brute pulled out a knife. Eyes wide, he rushed at me and cut the rope that bound my wrists. I'm not embarrassed to say that I was too shocked to flinch, which would have been my reaction if I had not been frozen in fear. Instead, I thanked the man and allowed him to help me up.

Standing sent blood back to parts of my legs that had been lacking. They tingled with pins and needles. I fluffed out my skirt, hoping I'd be able to walk—or run—if needed. "Now, if you give me my father, I will take you to the gold."

The door to the study banged open, and Finn entered with several police officers. They had weapons and leveled them at all gathered—including me!

Finn

"Move, and you're dead!"

My warning surprised everyone in Cornelius Abbot's study, especially Willa. Her eyes flashed at me, and I almost dropped my gun.

"Willa?" I choked out her name, not expecting to find her standing amongst them like a partner in crime. They'd snatched her off the street, or so witnesses had told me.

I'd called for the Land Officers, and we'd raided the home, hoping to save Willa from their clutches. Not surprisingly, she didn't need saving. If her expressive eyes were any indication, she wanted to throttle me for barging in and possibly ruining some plan she'd hatched.

A man stood next to her with a knife, and he was having none of my order. He launched toward me, blade headed for my heart. With his proximity so close to Willa, I could not shoot and risk harming her. Instead, I rushed forward, closing the distance, twisted to evade the weapon, and kicked the man's feet out from under him. He smacked into the floorboards with a devilish, satisfying crack.

I smiled at Willa, for not every lawman could handle himself so well, but she only yawned. Yawned!

"Oh, do take care," Willa cried out, having no thought for me. She bent to the man on the floor. "Dear me, your poor back. Can you move?"

She glanced back at me, and I could not fathom the emotion. I understood it. Don't get me wrong. Our uncanny ability to communicate without words still existed, but what she sent me was only venom. She wanted me to retreat and not harm the bastards that yanked her off the street like a bag of potatoes.

"Enough," the Land Officer said. I'd asked him for help—the same officer Willa lied to about her father's corpse. He stepped forward to take control.

After all, it was his city, and I was just a Pinkerton mucking around and possibly running out of my usefulness. He had the attitude of a man who would take no clues from me, let alone Willa. If my goal had been to come to her aid and not question her ways, I'd need to act fast or fail her. The Land Officer was about to throw the book at the lot of them.

"No one move," I repeated. "You will present Cornelius Abbot to this officer, or there will be Hell to pay."

Eyes shifted, and fingers pointed, but no one gave up the man.

Raising my gun, I fired a shot into the ceiling.

TWENTY

WILLA

"Where is Cornelius Abbot?"

The question came from the Land Officer this time. He once asked me to identify a dead body. By his sour expression, which skimmed right over me, he must have figured out that I could not be trusted. Not that I blamed him. I'd lied about one dead man's identity and just been found in the company of another man thought murdered. However, it wasn't my fault that Kansas City had a problem with the dead.

"Where's her father?" Finn clarified with an edge to his voice that should not be ignored.

Reggie Brown must have heard the threat, too. He nodded toward a mahogany wardrobe. One of the policemen went over and opened it, revealing an unconscious man inside.

A pang fluttered in my heart. It was Father! I wanted to go to him, but Finn moved forward and took my arm. He leaned close and whispered, "You can do nothing to help him. I implore you to retreat."

The policeman eased my father out of the wardrobe, eliciting a moan. I could breathe again, knowing he was alive. Until that moment, I barely had hold of my will, as it threatened to shatter. Finn's gentle words, however, lingered. I knew he meant well. Good men usually did.

Finn remained close, and I pulled at his lapel. The leather jacket was soft to the touch with a woodsy scent. I wanted to stand near him and breathe it in, but we only had a second. In my most earnest tone, I whispered, "Get my father and remove him to safety. Leave me with Reggie."

"I cannot!"

"You will," I kept my voice low and blunt, "if I mean anything to you."

My eyes flicked up to his as I tried to convey my plan—or at the very least that I had one—and his presence would ruin it.

Finn studied me briefly, cleared his throat, and stepped back. "Officer, Miss Abbot, and Mr. Brown have nothing to do with this matter. We'll take Mr. Abbot and the others for questioning."

The Land Officer shot Finn a look filled with questions that might cause a revolt. However, Finn didn't flinch. The officer nodded acceptance and signaled his men to comply. It was happening... my plan was coming together. Finn did as I asked. My heart swelled. Every indication told me he was a keeper.

Finn signaled for the Land Officer to clear the room. With one last desperate glance my way, he left, leaving me alone with the despicable Reggie Brown. The man who had used my father's identity to steal and undermine a whole town of respectable citizens looked smug by the turn of events. He considered me with a humorous glance. I had done the impossible—got him out of a police raid. He should have been a little impressed.

Instead, the cockney accent sounded exceptionally superior as Reggie turned to me. "What are you playing at, missy? I'm not some simple-minded sot. There ain't no gold, and while I do thank you for keeping me out of a cell, I don't need your tricks. Got my own. Your father's good name is still mine."

"Oh, the police aren't done with you. Did they give that impression? I assure you, the Pinkerton Man is itching for a chat," I countered.

He squared his shoulders but eased into one of the chairs facing the desk, all nonchalant. If I intimidated him, it didn't show. However, a redness piqued his cheeks.

I remained standing. To sit would feel like falling into a trap, which was not part of my plan. "Are you confused?" I asked. "Let me make one point crystal clear. I'll take the Abbot signet ring in exchange for the treasure map."

"The fake map." Reggie chuckled, shaking his head like he'd been left to babysit a problematic child. "The map, by the by, that I found in an old trunk and had doctored to look legit."

Pacing, I fed him back the same attitude. "Would you even know a real treasure map? Maybe you had one all along and didn't realize it because the map led me to runes carved in stone." As convincing as his forgery sounded, the map did reveal an ancient rune. He'd unknowingly done something right. Had the map led to all the runes and the Spanish gold? I'd not had time to ascertain that from Finn. "One rune is nearby in the bluffs; go look. Did your fake map maker carve that for you?" At his doubtful expression, I pressed on. "I think not. I think you conned people into a fake scheme with a real treasure map."

Hands on my hips, I hoped he felt the gravity of his mistake.

Reggie had heard enough. He surged up from his chair, glaring. "You don't seem to understand, missy." He moved toward me in that threatening way men exhibit when their size—in this case, girth—overshadowed another's. Luckily, I held something bigger and more powerful: my mind.

"You may have gotten your father away from me, but only in body. I have others that bear his continuance and can pass as him. Cornelius Abbot is mine and shall dance to my whim across this vast country. I shall not relinquish his signet ring." Reggie relished his position, puffing out his chest.

Proving he'd stolen my father's identity was a twisted kind of problem. If we were in New York, perhaps it would be easier, but the rarity of the crime meant educating the banks and police. A difficult task. I needed to stop Reggie's desire—and get the ring. My father habitually used it to sign his correspondence, pressing the ring's initials into hot wax. It was known, and if Reggie kept the ring, he could continue to usurp Father's identity.

Reggie snarled at me. "Oh dear, girl, whatever you believe, the reality is worse. I shall not leave you alone until you take me to the gold. Take care, as I am capable of doubling the shame upon your family."

I stuck my tongue out. "No."

"No?" Reggie blustered.

"You took two of Father's rings," I said. "I have one back, and you will see no gold until I have the other."

"Does your family name mean nothing to you?" Reggie scoffed. "I doubt you will make a good match if it is tarnished."

Of all the ways to bend me to his will, Reggie Brown picked the wrong one. I cared little for the marriage market. In fact, his threat had the opposite effect, and I laughed in his face.

"Oh my, you are so entertaining, sir, but I am growing weary." I redirected his focus. "I offer the map, and thus the Spanish gold, for my father's ring. No more, no less." I pointed outside the house to a distant location. "My roommate is waiting to bring it all to you. I have only to signal her that it is safe."

He went to the window. I doubted he could see far; darkness had taken over the night. Soft lights shone from the street and the homes beyond. They did little to abate the shadows, languishing in a welcoming stretch across the yard.

Seeing nothing, Reggie snarled at me. "I want the gold, not the map."

"Broaden your horizons, dear Reggie," I advised, surprised at his lack of vision. Being set in his way might just be his undoing. "Your scheme can be reproduced... if you have the map. Why would you only take the gold when the map is an investment in future dealings?"

Reggie's nose scrunched up. The wheels, while sluggish, turned. "You're a smarty pants, I must say."

"Think of it!" I painted the picture of future riches. "You have a real treasure map, and its authenticity is proven. It marks four spots around Kansas City. Think of the opportunities you have to multiply your riches by doing your dastardly deals with a real treasure map in your hands." My sweet smile softened the insult.

At least, it appeared to work its magic as dawning crept across Reggie's craggy face. "I accept. Signal your girl."

I shook a finger at him. "I'll have the ring first. You have not proven yourself trustworthy."

He grunted, almost sounding like he approved. "I do wonder why you did not sic your Pinkerton Man on me; perhaps Sullivan and Tuck were right about you."

I concealed my pleasure that con men Sullivan and Tuck had served me well. I'd hoped my "cooperation" with the duo would get back to Reggie. It certainly made him more accepting than I'd anticipated. He dug the gold signet ring out of an inner pocket hidden between his vest and hairy chest. He wiggled it into the palm of his hand and held it out to me.

Drawn to the ring, I moved closer. Granted, I'd been keeping my distance and held no delusion of wrestling it from him. He could clamp his hand shut and keep it from me. Nor were my thoughts on escaping if he chose to attack. I braced myself. For what? I did not know. I reached a hand out for the ring.

"The Pinkerton Man was an option," I admitted, "but I could not take the risk that you'd hidden the ring, but here you had it on you all along."

"Clever girl," he said. "But relinquishing the ring does not sever my ties with your father. Or... should I say your father's good name. I care not for his person and would appreciate you taking him back to New York City."

I nodded, agreeing that Reggie had already set up enough connections, using my father's solid business reputation. Losing the signet ring would slow the extent of the damage and perhaps allow Father to send out letters to warn friends and banks, but significant harm had been done. It could take years to be free.

One problem at a time, I told myself.

With quick fingers, I snatched the gold signet ring from Reggie's sweaty hand. I was fast—but he was quicker. His beefy hand wrapped around my wrist and held tight. The iron grasp stalled any efforts to move away as pain shot up my arm.

"Send the signal," he hissed.

Our eyes locked, and his intent was so clear I knew he would not let me leave with the ring—or my life. Darkness hovered within his soul, making me gasp. I never had a chance with Reggie, not from our first meeting on the train when he appeared as a helpful friend of my father's.

It struck me that I'd fallen into his trap from the very beginning. The realization chilled my soul.

Twenty-One

WILLA

"Send the signal."

Reggie Brown's order held a sour note. It hinted at physical harm, a threat compounded by the tight grip he had on my wrist.

My heart raced. I'd misjudged the lengths he'd reach to maintain his con. To me, it all seemed to be slipping out of his grasp. The police were on to him, and he'd grossly mismanaged the map. I honestly thought he'd cut and run at the first opportunity. Yet, I'd been wrong. Something darker lurked in his soul, and he'd not be undone by a girl.

I tried to avoid his eyes. A soulless hunger shone from their depths, and standing so close was all I could handle.

He reeked of anxious sweat. "I need to light a candle and place it in the window," I said.

Reggie grinned. It revealed too many teeth. His head cocked toward the nearest window, indicating where we'd move. He had no intention of releasing me to perform the task.

With my free hand, I transferred Father's ring away from Reggie and slipped it into my skirt pocket. He could always take it off my dead body, but he'd have to search for it. I'd not make it easy for him, for clearly, he lusted after all the available treasure—and my father's signet ring was one. All he needed to continue the farce of being Cornelius Abbot was a man who fit Father's general description and the ring. It would seal any deal.

Reggie jerked me toward the window, allowing me to snatch a candlestick along the way. "I'll need both hands to light it," I said, and he released me. My fingers barely cooperated, but the candle flame finally licked to life.

I placed the candlestick on the window sill. It was one of two large windows that faced the front wrap-around porch. The light would be visible from the street.

"Now we wait," I whispered.

Reggie grunted, grasping my wrist again. The pressure was less, but it still kept me near him. "Your father may lose all he holds dear when it comes to his reputation and wealth," Reggie said with some satisfaction, "but he will always be rich with a daughter like you."

I frowned at the compliment, but before I could send him a withering stare, footsteps thudded up the mansion's front steps. The sound echoed to us, even as the front door banged open.

Reggie frowned. "Not a dainty little lady, eh?" His eyebrows rose, although he had no hairline to hide under.

"We're in here!" I shouted.

Reggie allowed the summons. "Yes, come on in like a lamb to the slaughter," he half-joked.

The joke, however, was on him. A flood of Harvey Girls entered the room, led by Dori and Mrs. Agnes Q. Downs. Shocked, Reggie relaxed his grip even more, and I pulled my arm free, able to move away and join my friends. More Harvey Girls approached the windows as they crowded onto the porch outside.

"Wha-what is this?" he stuttered, confidence quickly draining. It left him looking like a howl-faced ghoul.

"It's the Harvey Girls," Dori said sweetly.

"We're fetching the police, as well," Mrs. Downs added. "We wouldn't want to leave a man like you wandering the streets of our fine city."

"I doubt the police went far," I said, "or my Pinkerton Man." I winked at Dori, more than pleased that she had followed my plan and brought the 'calvary' with her.

"Never underestimate a lady's power, Mr. Brown, when she's backed by her sisters."

"If it's the last thing I do, I shall get even with you, Willa Abbot!" Reggie's empty threat was met with girlish laughter.

I'm happy to report that the Harvey Girls' show of force was the talk of Kansas City. We'd secured our place in town by aiding in the apprehension of a notorious con man. Reggie Brown would not be fooling anyone again anytime soon. Although, he reluctantly went to jail, bemoaning how I'd double-crossed him by keeping all the Spanish gold for myself.

I explained the map and the runes to the authorities. The stone carvings proved the gold had been hidden at one time, but I firmly believe the Spanish soldiers would never have left it behind. Yes, many were slaughtered at the time, but I chose to believe they sacrificed themselves so a small group could escape with the riches. Of course, we may never know.

Finn's trip was only a minor success. He found the other runes, but they meant nothing when the sketches were all studied together. Dori claimed most treasure maps were made to deceive. Thieves rarely trusted enough to leave a clear path to their treasure.

I was happy to put Spanish gold and treasure hunting behind me and reunite with my father. He needed to convalesce. Since he had a house in town—even though Reggie had purchased it for him—it was his, and he took refuge there. His jovial lust for life soon returned. I visited with him, naturally, but I'd become attached to the Harvey House and its crew. Plus, I'd signed a contract and was determined to honor it.

Shortly after our triumph, Mrs. Agnes Q. Downs summoned me to her office. The excitement over the Harvey Girls assembling to save the day was still high and had brought extra guests to the Harvey House. Thus, I felt confident the matron would only praise me, but a quiver of fear lingered. Mrs. Downs was a stern woman. I dared not assume she condoned all my actions.

True to form, Mrs. Downs greeted me with a grunt and a frown. I took the offered chair, placing my hands in my lap. I'd seen my mother assume the contrite position before. It usually worked for her. Of course, she'd never tried to stop a scoundrel and thus endanger all her friends.

"You'll be leaving us," Mrs. Downs said.

My shock must have shown on my face. I was speechless as the news took the wind out of me.

"Now, don't tell me we'll need the smelling salts," Mrs. Downs chuckled. "You're made of sturdier stuffin', and you'll need it. Mr. Harvey has a special mission for you."

I sat forward, intrigued. "How can I help Mr. Harvey?"

"Due to your unique skills," Mrs. Downs cleared her throat, unwilling to name said skills, "Mr. Harvey believes you can tame some of the unruly spots that pop up, occasionally, along the whole Harvey House line. As such, you will be his Ambassador, traveling to any Harvey House that needs you to calm a prickly situation."

I sat back, so pleased by the idea of sticking my fingers into trouble—and fixing it—that I could barely contain my joy. "Oooh," I sighed, "I believe I am up for such a challenge."

Mrs. Downs smirked. I gathered that she knew full well she'd given me a job full of adventure—and that I'd take to it with glee. "You will be taking the other one with you, too."

"The other one?" I choked out the question.

"Your roommate, Dori Hilbert." Mrs. Downs shook her head. "One lady alone is not respectable."

"But two poking around is perfectly fine?" I teased, having no problem with her choice of companion. Dori was indispensable and wise in ways I never would be. Plus, she'd become the dearest friend in the shortest amount of time.

Mrs. Downs leaned forward, perhaps sensing a need to reprimand me. "Don't embarrass us."

"Of course not," I promised.

Before I knew it, I'd sent Father back to New York City into the loving care of my mother and boarded a train in the opposite direction. A Harvey House needed us, and all haste was required in time to right a wrong. As Dori and I settled into the first-class coach, we were joined by one more traveler intent on aiding our journey—Finn Morgan.

Wearing a new bowler hat, the Pinkerton Man sauntered towards our seats, indicating his intention to join our party. Since he'd proven to be exceptionable at following my plan to save Father despite having misgivings, I smiled at his arrival. He'd be a welcome addition.

"Please, have a seat," I said, as we'd taken up a space with two backward seats facing two forward ones. It offered a bit of privacy. "Do tell us how lucky we are to have a Pinkerton Man join our little team."

He winked, sitting next to Dori and looking happier than I'd ever seen him. Well, not as happy as when I'd led Reggie Brown and the army of Harvey Girls to the police station. He'd been waiting a block away and looked rather astonished.

"Mr. Harvey insisted," Finn explained.

"How kind," I said, sitting across from my friends. I tried to recall how much excitement a lady should show at a man's arrival. I must have missed that etiquette class, but probably no more than a pleased glance.

Dori whooped her approval. "We never did hear about your search for the Spanish runes. Was it as fraught with danger as the first one?"

Finn put his feet up on the open seat next to me, closing his eyes and pulling his hat down to protect them from the light. "Oh, I cannot talk about that; I'm sorry to inform you."

"I'm certain there's nothing to tell," I insisted.

"Unless..," Dori considered all the possibilities, "he doesn't want to tell us because he really did find the Spanish treasure, and now he's rich!" Dori clapped her hands together.

Finn grunted. "If I'd found the gold, we'd be riding in first class."

"We are riding in first class!" Dori exclaimed.

Finn only smiled, getting comfortable in his seat. He settled in for a long journey.

"He didn't find the gold," I hissed.

Dori only hummed a little tune. She didn't really care. I pushed Finn's feet off the seat, and his smile grew. I really wanted to see his eyes under that hat brim, for they must be gleeful. He had some nerve, telling such a fib. He really was insufferable.

Finn cleared his throat. "Have you heard this one?" he asked. "A Pinkerton Man and two Harvey Girls board a train..."

"No, what happens?" Dori asked, as innocent as ever.

I patted Dori's knee before settling back in my seat as well. "Don't you worry; we'll figure out the ending to that sentence soon enough."

Finn tipped his hat up and winked at me.

The End

NEXT

The Harvey Girl Continues

The next part of *The Harvey Girl* is coming. The story is serialized first on Substack by **Tell Me A Mystery**, where there's tons of thrilling mysteries to read. Discover more at https://linktr.ee/tellmeamystery

ABOUT THE AUTHOR

Ann Kimbrough spends her days writing suspenseful stories dipped in history, magic and mystery. You can find her on Substack as Tell Me a Mystery, where she serializes mysteries for fans to read, along with short audio mysteries—entertainment for the ears. Find information and links to all her books at https://linktr.ee/tellmeamystery

Some of Ann's Other Book Series:

Cozy Mysteries—The Fit Girls series—on Amazon under pen name Ann Audree. A fitness instructor travels to high-end resorts and stumbles into trouble—and a murder to solve.

Paranormal Mysteries —*The Time Witch*—serialized on Substack. A magical world surprised a young woman trying to open a B&B in an old Carnegie library.